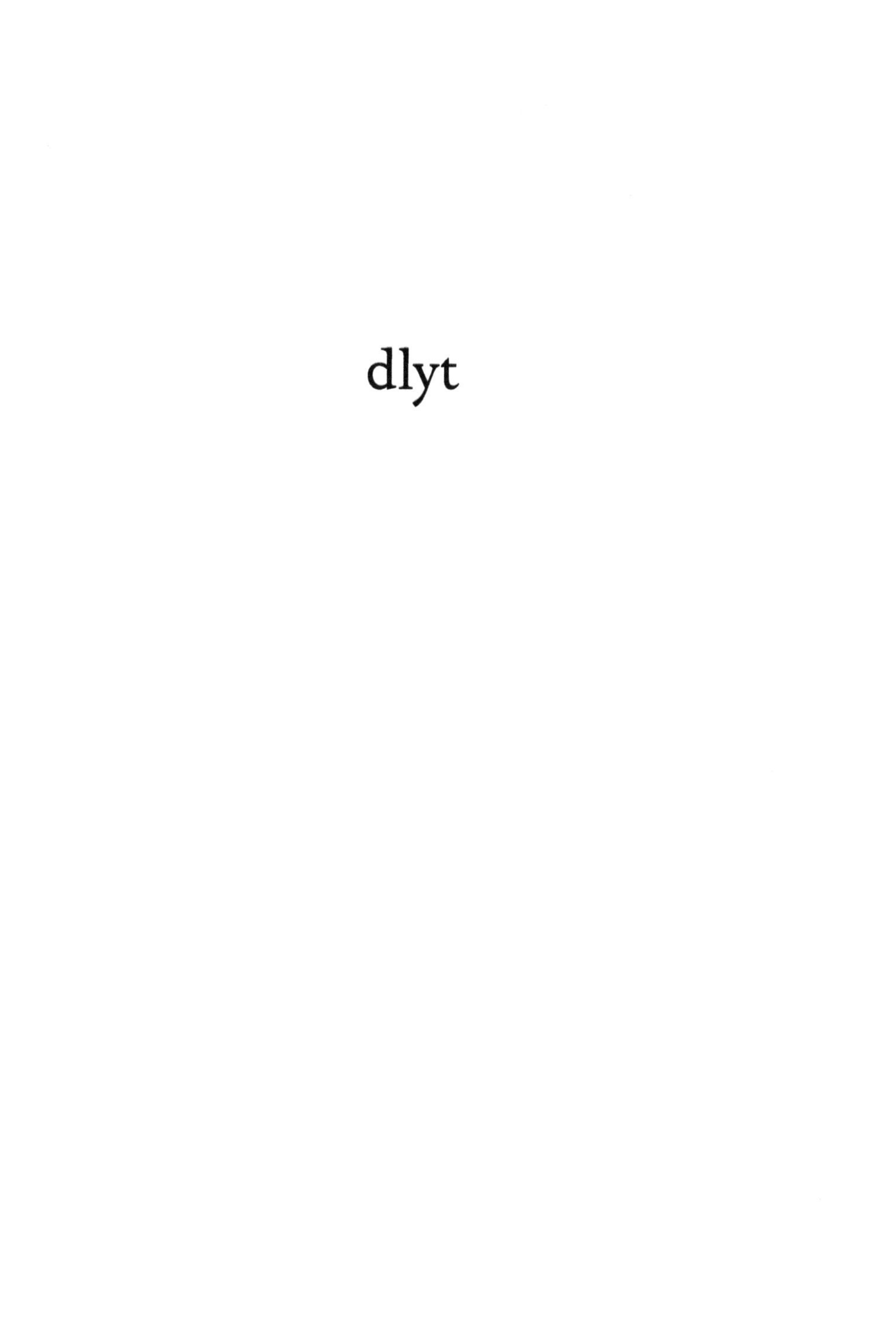
dlyt

dlyt

Roc Sandford

Gometra 2021

This edition was set in Eric Gill's
72, 24, 20, 18, 12, 11, 10 & 9 point
Golden Cockerel by Roc Sandford on May Day, 2021
Printed and bound by IngramSpark
Cloth cover 978-1-900389-04-4
Paperback 978-1-900389-06-8
This is number
of an edition of
copies

To the dogs!

I believe that as a rule one should read only those books that sting and prick the conscience. If the book we are reading doesn't wake us up with a smack in the head, then why read it? So it'll make us happy, as you write? My God, what would make us happy would be just to have no books at all, the kind of books that make us happy if we have to we can write ourselves. The books we need, however, are those which affect us like a painful misfortune, like the death of somebody dearer to us than ourselves, like being driven out into the woods away from all people, like a suicide, a book should be the axe for the frozen sea within us.
(Kafka, letter to a friend, 1904.)

Pride yourself, writer! You have dug-up your deepest shames, you have cast them from you. And now, changed into a *zone of subculture*, your dustbin has become your claim to fame.
(Gombrowicz, *A Kind of Testament.)*

One should never be afraid to go too far for the truth lies beyond.
(Proust, letter to a friend, 1921.)

Although the sharpest judges of the witches, and even the witches themselves, were sure of the guilt of witchcraft, the guilt nevertheless did not exist. All guilt is like that.
(Nietzsche, *The Gay Science.)*

I'd need three military bands to give the impression of silence in music. (Cabaner.)

Contents

Foreword

> All wished to leave this drying crust,
> borne on the delicate wings of lust
> like bees, and cast their fertile drop
> into the overwhelming cup.
> (Lowell, *Central Park.*)

A love of mine once said to me—*There was an escaped horse on the roundabout running the wrong way. It reminded me of you.*

There is an element of *running the wrong way* to these stories, written when I was younger.

Cynopolis

> Deliver my soul from the sword;
> my darling from the power of the dog.
> Save me from the lion's mouth:
> for thou hast heard me
> from the horns of the unicorns.
> *(Psalm 22, King James Version.)*

Moving slowly at first, so as not to dent our shining wings, we came in amongst what looked like icebergs floating in slushy water and throbbing from within with sliding green & blue lights. The sun flickered and began to strobe, and through the crazed perspex of the porthole, our wings were dulled. The clouds lost their edge and turned to mist, and the mist submerged us. We flew faster. Then the seatbelt-sign came up and the aircraft burped and rumbled in the hollow parts beneath our feet.

—Wheels, said my neighbour from the darkness of the cabin and I turned to him and answered.
—Yes.

Beneath us was a lower surface, like cold water on which snow has fallen. Deep beneath that, the darkening landscape trembled, still stained with pools of tainted light where the waterlogged & sinking sun, under its hot-pink woollen lid, glowed in from the sea. We saw cars moving on a freeway with their headlamps lit, but also the organised shadows of trees, a brown castle, the rails of a railway catching horizontal apricot sunlight, and the muscular, blinding coils of the river. Then the city itself, passing quickly underneath us, see-thru as the innards of a prawn—pumping, whirring, rocking, clicking—until we crossed the coast and were out over lurid breakers.

The foil of my neighbour's complimentary peanut packet refused to yield, until it suddenly split, spraying peanuts.

—Whoops, he stated, with a flash of his steel-rims.
—Don't mention it, I said.

Out at sea we banked, wings vibrating, and glided low over wrinkled waves, amongst the scabbed and rusting ships, and back across a band of marbled surf, grateful, towards the runway.

Peanut-man had taken the packet between his lips and was using it as a kazoo.

—Oh! Excuse me, he said.
—Not at all.

Through the porthole, as we sank amongst derelict aircraft & hangars, I saw a minute dog, trotting through the dust, its trotting shadow blue with a hang-dog head and dangling tongue. It sat abruptly to rest, raised its muzzle towards us, tilted its face to take in this grating apparition floating slowly by. Then opened its mouth sharply three times, each time recoiling. And then away and running with the beast! But unable to keep up, even in parallax, it fell rapidly back, and was obscured almost immediately by our fancy wingtip fin.

I took a taxi from the airport.

—*Soy optimista,* the driver told me, gesturing with both hands at the national colours adorning the sky, beyond the rim of cloud, in sharp bands of yellow and red. That was on one side of the moving taxi; on the other it was night.
—Yes?
—*Sí, soy optimista.*
—Then I'm glad.
—*Sí, gracias.*

Our road skirted the airport. After a reddish-blue forest came corroded hills, encrusted with minerals leaking from the soil. Sour, lamp-lit factories lined the highway and vented tumbling volumes of steam and thin, whistling jets of coloured smoke. We crossed a foamy river overhung by sticky black trees, and a swelling heath where undulating strands of toilet paper snagged on clumps of myrtle and esparto grass. The rushing traffic thickened and congealed, closed-in behind, and dazzled us with red and yellow lamps.

—*¿Le gusta la musica?*, the driver was asking me as, gazing down benignly from his rear-view mirror, he tuned the dashboard radio, panning across the stations and the gaps of crackle in-between. We heard snaps of conversation, lost chords, the suggestive enthusiasm of advertisements, the martial bands whose function they've displaced, tinny pop, & static. Yet all these sounds had unexpected unity, like a careful modern composition.

—He like music?, he asked again.

Through the plastic air-vents came air which smelt of vinegar and tasted of gin. Rhythmic silver streetlight fell on the banks of the road, on dented wash-machines, scattered rubble, and the tilted orange shells of burnt-out cars.

The flicking neon of a row of cheap, suggestive, one-night hotels showed on ahead, approached, coloured up our faces, and flowed into the past.

—*Deutsche, ja?* my driver was asking me.
—*Entschuldigung, nein.*
—*Kein Problem.*

And, amongst a scatter of eroded high-rise blocks, moulded in concrete by playful hands, and graced with a bunting of stiffening underwear, the traffic squealed and panted as—our lane burning with a brake-light which was all the same exuberant light, glowing behind a fretted mask to represent, like a painting on backlit glass, the textured freeway and the nominal cars—we stopped.

With an idiot joy through the windscreen I saw up ahead the dog, the self-same dog!

A faded mongrel, wearing a winning white patch over one eye, it trotted spry along the freeway's bank, investigating weeds, turds and the odd ripped shoe. The lofty, aerial universe of foam and cloud and light-stained cityscape I had watched, as we sank, through my crazed porthole—with its phased reveal of fly-overs, sewerage works, banks of dying asphodel—was fused with the clogged world I now rode through, sharing as they did this very dog.

We must already have struggled for miles through stop-go traffic, yet still had not detached ourselves cleanly from the orbital fence of the airport And this more a comment on *being* itself, even of logic, of possibility, than an incident of metropolitan design.

As the blockage gave and the neighbouring lane began to roll, the mongrel braced itself on splayed legs to bark into menacing darkness lurking beyond the berm. Pausing to tilt its head and listen, it barked some more. Then reversed over a fragment of brick and swung *his* hind-leg up towards a tarnished moon already wobbling as it rose. A small spurt of urine dripped from the clump of whiskers at the base of his belly and sprinkled the dust. Already slipping into the past as we too got underway, he shivered sensuously, wagged his tail experimentally like a pilot testing a rudder flap, snapped out one precise final bark, and trotted onto the road. I had to twist awkwardly in the taxi's back-seat to see. A dull red sedan coming up the middle lane braked, missed, he trotted on. A pale blue coupé lurched to swipe, and flung him spinning fast but also turning slowly, spot-lit by yellow headlamps, in a high arc across the set.

As he span, he became a being not of desire, but shocked passivity, with no agency of his own. I saw him freeze-framed, cheeks flapping, displaying black gums, his back curled and hind-legs crossed as if reclining on an easy chair, and his pink & useless nipples improperly disclosed.

He landed with no bouncing and lay easy in the outside lane, his pelt lit by glaring brake-light, gnawing softly at a hooked paw. Revolving his eyes to my moonlike features, pressed against the cab's side window, he took me in with a tired, heartfelt gaze, swallowed with emotion, and tentatively moved his tail. With padded click a silver hatchback whirled him along the supple tarmac between its wheels in a plump, furred tube of testicles and teeth. Our lane too began again to roll. The dog was keeled to one side, the stump of tail swinging loose. He was panting through black lips, his lower jaw pushed forwards, his fur scuffed and backcombed and his patience running out. I saw him bare his teeth and snap at its chunky treads as a tyre ran up between his outstretched legs and crunched across his belly. His hide inflated and his anal sphincter gave, and liquid and intestine snaked bubbling through the pink kiss at the root of his tail. The cars behind were honking for us to move, but before we moved my driver turned stiffly back towards me with dumb-bell lips, his face the colour of gravel and wet as if rinsed in water, glaring blindly through egg-white eyes. Then grinding his teeth like gears, we lurched off, leaving the bewildered dog leaking on soiled tarmac as with a double rhythm, like a heartbeat, warm motorists ramped over grating bones and on, into the city.

We'd dawdled so long in sclerotic traffic that the hotel kitchen was closed. All that could be done was a sweaty-cheese roll and a bottle of *San Miguel,* also perspiring, which I bore over billowing red carpets to the saloon. When it came to it I couldn't touch the cheese. Something in its texture spoke to me of dog.

Walled with splotched and yellowing mirrors and feigned marble, the saloon was the *belle époch's* last stand. The ceiling was painted with imitation clouds, and beneath them floated planes of cigarette-smoke. If these remained, all smokers but one had gone. Lacquer card-tables with moth-eaten baize were each set with a used glass ashtray and four bentwood chairs. There were no windows, but there were curtains, with lights behind simulating daylight when even now, outside, near here, it was night.

The lone smoker watched a bullfight on TV. She wore white boot-cut *Levis* with an ironed crease and, under them, polished black boots with the raked heel of a sailing boat. Slumped uncomfortably on her chair, with her head half hanging over the back, one of her ankles rested on the other knee and, at the scary parts, for bull at least, she picked rapidly at the label on her *San Miguel.* I couldn't see her face, but her hair fell back from a fish-tailed green ribbon and swung loose in flickering cascades. She wore a flimsy washed-out tartan shirt.

I could tell right away she was here to learn me the anguish of the dispossessed.

Carrying cheese and *San Miguel* through aquarium light to the table next to hers, I stared too at the TV. Rapt by her bullfight, she didn't look round. We were just too far apart to touch but it felt, with our faces in parallel, bathed in the light of the same pulsing screen, that the hot skin of her cheek was laid against mine, turning it cold.

When I spoke she gave me a dirty look and exhaled twin squirts of smoke. But I saw for the first time in my life her face, which turned me away, fogged my eyes and slowly ballooned my lungs.

She scared me! And as I spoke again my smile was more a drawing back of lips over teeth than a smile. She turned back towards me with ostentatious boredom but after a pause she placidly answered my question, whatever that was.

—I have absolutely *no* idea, she said.

We sat in silence for a time while I gazed at her, and with a faint ferocity she gazed not at the bullfight happening within it, now, but at the television set itself.

—Do me a favour, don't be a pain in the asshole, she added eventually, without moving her eyes from the screen.

—*Ass*, I corrected. And if anyone is being a pain in the ass, it's you.

This was a revelation she needed time to consider.

—It's you, not me, I added.

Not a good start.

At last she looked at me, holding my eyes fiercely and making hers fume. But as she shifted her chair away with a sudden jerk of her body there was the briefest treble flash of white, from between her lips and her eyelids, which she was gripping her lower lip with her teeth to suppress.

—And anyhow, why are you laughing?

She out-stared at me to prove she wasn't. Her cheeks were scooped under her cheek bones. Smudges under her eyes. Pale lips, with no brown or red in them but only, by the jumpy light of the bullfight and the steady neon of simulated day, the baby-pink of marshmallow. And her eyes ultramarine, with navy blue rings dividing the whites from the irises, where minute twists of marmalade drifted. I was looking at, not into her eyes, but I couldn't not. The two colours in her face, baby blue and baby pink, resonated behind their torn veil of exhaled smoke.

—If I'm such a pain in the asshole.

But something in her gave the game away by making her half-smile just as she asserted—

—I'm not laughing.

We endured another pause.

—But I saw you.
—Saw me what?, she asked, properly antagonistic and in no way smiling now.

I sweated like cheese.

She plonked down the glass she had taken up and scraping her chair round slightly showed me her teeth in what was supposed to be a noxious smile.

—You think that you are so cute!, she said, oscillating her face.

And jerking her chair with a screech my way, she leaned in and pressed her pointed finger, through clothing, against my ribcage at the level of my nipple. She twisted it like a gimlet to bore at just the place where it was being battered from inside by my heart.

—*Chistoso,* not *guapo,* she clarified, with her upper lip lifted from her teeth.

I didn't know what she meant.

—It's just I needed to talk, I clarified in turn. I couldn't not.
—But not to me!
—But yes, to you.
—Satisfied?
—Not yet.
—Shush! she said, lifting her eyebrows high in joyous disbelief not at me, but at creepiness itself.

Then, with a bob of her forehead and a wink on that side she indicated the glum waiter, monitoring us through one of the circular windows set in the double doors to the kitchen. As we both turned our faces to him, he dropped comically downwards out of sight.

—I'd like to know what you're like.
—I am what I look like, she said with forced asperity.

In reply I blankened what had been too beseeching a face, and she looked perplexed.

—Keep taking the *Prozac,* I said.
—What on earth do you mean?
—I mean forget it!

She turned away abruptly so that all I could see was her pale, burning hair gathered-in by its fish-tail ribbon, and the scooped side of her cheek, shining with the shifting light of the bullfight.

I took up my glass and saw her take up hers. We watched the bull choose its *querencia* and, stamping split hooves and puffing smoke, prepare to prevail.

—Only, I don't think I can, I added. Forget it, I mean.
—Fuck off, she said quietly, without turning round.
—Well, I can't. Not yet.
—Well you will have to try to do it. Unless I shall?

And she shook the last drips of *San Miguel* decisively into her glass.

We interrupted a long silence to each return the stare of the sullen waiter who, back behind his disk of bright window, with its backdrop of tiles and hanging implements, faltered, quailed, and again dropped comically out of sight.

—*I want to know what you're like!*

She was mocking me by playing back my lines in an odious voice while shaking her face and looking away from me.

—*Forget it!*

Without showing her face.

—*Only I can't!*

Her head rocking as she spoke. But her voice wasn't cold. She didn't seem capable of making it that. It had the same tone as when you blow on the mouth of a left-over *Coca-Cola* bottle, flat but sweet and warm, with low harmonics. A voice without expression in the sense that, although by its timbre it suggested affection and warmth, it did so whatever she might be saying. With a yelp from her chair she had turned her body to face me and was staring at me now with a small hostile face.

I smiled at her.

—*Well I can't, not yet!* she said, mocking me again in her flat, warm voice.

It was as if she was holding broken glass in her mouth, delicately so as not to cut herself. She talked from the back teeth.

—What's your name? I asked.

Suddenly she lifted the flat of her hand to palm her temple, mussed her hair and, shaking her face slowly, turned her eyes up to a painted sky, to cigarette clouds.

—He's absolutely impossible! she said, and bringing her eyes down to her *San Miguel* bottle, resumed urgently scraping the label.
—Maybe? Who knows.
—Maybe *not!* After emphasising *not* she kept her mouth tubed and eyes wide and looked from side to side. Then straightened up her back, turning her lower lip white by biting it. And then her eyes turned up to me, reflecting the light shallowly, so you couldn't see in.

Something amused her but she still tried not to smile.

Time passed.

—Not so chatty now? she asked. Something wrong?

And she couldn't avoid smiling, and then finally she even laughed. She showed her even, off-white teeth. The angles of her eyes changed and became part of one fixed arc.

— Less full of yourself at last?

Drained, I only wanted to shut mine.

Above us, televised, the bull died. When I didn't laugh back or answer, she stood and picked at the thighs of her white jeans. She bent down, facing away, to pull them down the outside of her boots.

—I am going now. Bye-bye.

And over her head she pulled a white mannerist turtle-neck, tugging the fluffy sleeves until they covered the backs of her hands.

—When can we meet? I asked faintly.

She made a face, let it drop, and walked out. Glum as the waiter, slumped in my bentwood chair, my eyes had half-closed when, from behind me, someone shoved me. She was holding out a scrap of quivering newspaper in an otherwise steady hand. I looked up at her face, then down at an integer written there. She didn't smile.

—Maybe tomorrow, she said. We can see. We could go out. *Maybe.*

Then she turned and engaged with an over-long vista of red carpet which, as she receded, she seemed to ascend like a steep slope in an oncoming gale. And I watched her struggle through the stiff revolving door which, at first resisting, then ejecting her unexpectedly, made her run a few steps towards the backed-up traffic with her fingers splayed.

On the TV screen the bull was dragged over sand, a crumpled, stiffening, bull-skin rug. I, too, felt like that. Shattered, I couldn't sleep. My room droned all night like the cabin of the airliner. It was the kitchen's vents. After breakfasting alone & haggard in that same saloon—I was, it seemed, the sole guest— I called her from a gilded telephone-booth under the polished brass staircase of the hotel.

—Is Ana there? I had to shout above the vicious crackling of the line.
—*¿Sí?* asked a faint, humourless voice, perhaps her landlady.
—Is Ana there?
—Yes, I am Ana.

She sounded disappointed that I'd called, was waiting for me to speak.

—Remember me?
—*¡Eres un jodido idiota!* But of course!
—Would you like to go out sometime?

Another silence.

—Would you?
—I do not know, she said in a high, dispassionate voice, as if pointed out a distant object of little interest to her. I'm busy now. And tired. I couldn't sleep. Call me later, if you like to.

And so, later—a triple avenue of cranes, palms and telegraph poles rimmed the harbour-front, which had something unconscionable but sad about it.

Faded, flesh-pink marble blocks, laid to contain an otherwise vaguely transgressive sea, were scuffed and tacky with oil-stains. Hot sunlight fell on these through freezing air.

A flight of steps led underwater, inviting us to descend and amble amongst bottles, a sunken motorbike and the twisted frame of a pram, all grained and camouflaged in the slowly undulating bluish-green light of the harbour-bed.

Fish disguised as sodden newsprint were grazing there. These scattered as a boat rattled by, its syncopated engine-beat followed by the organic noise of waves slapping pink stone.

Ana's colours were washed-out in the thin sunlight. Her hair, which had been a ringletted reddish blonde, had become dull, wavy and curled. Perhaps she'd shampooed it. And her eyes were now more grey than blue or jade, and the colour of her lips didn't jar her disk-like face, whitish, as her lipstick had last night.

Whether, having been given the wrong number, I had got the wrong girl, or the light of the bullfight on TV had deceived me—I don't know.

The zoo was a false start. The scabby lion in his concrete pit was able to implicate but not scare us. Her head began to jerk, her cheeks went red, she dabbled with tears.

—Tragic! she kept saying as we walked.

Her nose ran. But eventually she turned, her face tilted slightly downwards and then, looking seriously up at me, put her hand over her mouth. Her skin lay across her cheeks and her nose without a crease, which gave a bluntness to her features, moulded, not carved or sketched.

—Super tragic! she repeated.
—What is?
—A lion in a city. Like us!
—A lion should be in a Giorgione or Titian, in a Stubbs, I told her. Not a zoo.
—Not in a zoo, she assented, but where it really lives.

Suitably dismayed by the zoo, we turned out through gleaming turnstiles towards a forked pylon, propping the middle of the sagging cord which was slung like a washing-line between opposing city-clad hills and bore an ancient cable-car back and forth.

A hand-written notice was attached with strands of pink wool to the pylon's base.

¡Vols barats sobre la ciutat!

it proclaimed in loopy breathlessness, and we each, singly, paid our fares to be drawn slowly upwards through a rotting mesh of cast-iron struts and braces, caked in a dried red foam of rust. Ana looked disturbed.

—I doesn't like this, she said.
—Should it fall, it's just like any lift, you just jump as we hit bottom.
—No, it's moving, she squeaked.

The whole flat sea, seen through a sinking fretwork, ever renewed, of blackish-red triangles, rose slowly, first to one side of the shuddering, dangling lift, then to the other, and placing both hands on one of my shoulders, she wrapped one leg around my leg whilst, her head ducked and resting on my chest, she squinted upwards. She made me stagger, and not with her weight.

—Well, if we fall in the water, remember not to speak—a fish might swim in.
—We're swinging, she was saying in a taut voice, and tried to laugh.

Her face was grey and had sweat on it, and where she gripped my shoulders it hurt.

—What happened to your fire? I asked. It turned to water! And this is just a lift. God knows how you'll take the cable car!

Using her chin, I tilted her face up. Her wet grey eyes were looking downwards, then they too came up, slightly crossed, like a dolly who's been knocked on the head.

—You're alright, I told her, and her body softened. She nodded, unhooked her leg from mine, and looked mournfully at the cigarette stubs, some still smoking, smeared across the floor, while moving her lips fast and silently, a girl who'd been subtly wronged.

—The fairest tree in the forest, overnight, became a vine, I said.
—Isn't funny, she said, in a dark voice.

When the lift stopped and its greased, concertina gates clashed open, she shuffled cautiously out onto a viewing platform whose balustrade, like something out of Jules Verne, was formed in woven wicker, and turned to me her earnest face.

—Be proud of me. I kept my cool, she said. If anything could be worse than the zoo, it is that.

The cocktail of boredom, fear and joy which constitutes paradise.

—You see, I want to tell you that today, I gave up cigarettes and coffee. That was meeting, was meeting you, last night, she said. Meeting you, she said.

I had to think deeply about that.

Above us a yellow wheel revolved, dabbed with dobs of scalloped grease, and pierced with cut-out discs of varying diameters. A slack hawser was yanked and tightened, the wicker creaked and the ironwork sang. The wheel screeched and lowed as piteously as an *abattoir*. Telling not only of *dog*, but more.

And as for the pile-driver out in the harbour with its hiss and visceral thuddings—because they were extending the mole—like a lost word or an unremembered dream, my mind hid and taunted me with whatever it was that *that* spoke.

A minute cable-car in racing-green bounced from a hole far away on a ragged hill. And whirred towards us dancing under the hawser. Until, squealing routinely now, more aviary than slaughterhouse, the turning yellow wheel slowed. The car, like a comical gondola shorn of its Zeppelin, bumped the rubbed wooden guides on our tower and floated in to dock. Above us an ultra-stiff pulse rippled in a complex and gigantic spring, smeared with vibrating feathers.

With something of a magnetic reluctance on her part, which held her for a moment in the doorway, unable to enter, we embarked.

The interior of the aerial car, formed in *Bakelite* and a delaminating burr-walnut veneer, its mauve banquets leaking their off-white wadding, had the air of the cheapest box at a shuttered opera.

The attendant, in a striped shirt and beribboned beret, smelt like a handful of dirty coins.

Closing the doors with a ring and a clump without looking up from her auto-magazine, and beginning sensuously and unconsciously to itch and probe and even excavate her crack, she, the attendant, moved her fingers beneath the stiff back-pockets of dirt-glazed blue-jeans, pausing only to gnaw a shivered fingernail, broken in sufficiently nasty a way, when you looked at it, for you to feel hurt.

—Gross! lip-synched Ana.

She leant back against the closed door, her arms folded, pointedly insouciant but twisting her lip and frowning. Then she softened her face, and her lips and eyes rippled. There was a pause of half a heartbeat, and we began to whirr and swing. To one side of the flimsy car, the remote suburban mountains, clothed in glossy shrubs, rose and fell like lungs; to the other the dusty, thrilling plane of the sea tilted, inflated, slid as, bouncing and swaying, we journeyed solemn above the city.

But the air around our gondola was darkened by an immense cloud of what at first looked like locusts but turned out to be birds. A swarm, lobed and pulsing like a heart, distended *and* stretched, revolving in spirals invisible to us, like those of a galaxy viewed from within—contracting *and* shrinking, even shrivelling, before re-inflating and unexpectedly reversing in space or time. It turned this juddering car; and the slack black helical wire from which it hung; plus the scabbed plane trees of the central square with their big foolish bright-green leaves sprouting in bunches like something nice for a salad conveyed, erratic and tempting, just beneath our bouncing, jubilant feet; together with that temporarily earthbound reflection in the pickled surface of some euphoric lake of our own slung gondola—a tram!, chattering and ringing on polished rails, spumes of fizzling white sparks cascading around it like the veils of a bride—what was this—a festival of nineteenth century transports—of wicker, pitch-pine, brass? And the dusty, melted, questing, organic forms of the apartment buildings; and the stick-people on-the-move down their clogged trails, with tinny limbs and enormous heads, rearing, clothed, clustering too on *café* terraces for grains of sugar and minute stoops of glistening fluid, some resinous emanation of the tables themselves, observed by us as they slid below and yet seeming uncaring, as if we, who were *everything*, meant nothing to them, such was our shaking & shrieking stealth;—all this was simply an elaborate instrument or observatory or even institution, dedicated to conjuring up and then gazing complacent and stunned at the whirling, looming, squirting, speckled fountains of starlings, those wings of being itself—the secret of the speckles on the feathers of each bird being that it is the hidden-in-plain-view map of its own station and trajectory in the starling-cloud—at the centre of all of which, flickering and fly, like candles melting one-another because placed too close, our hands fanned beside our faces on grubby plate-glass, our breath (as the ferocious evening-breezes panted) for the first time misting it—comprehensively moved and touched and elevated, reminded of our centrality to that which is, all of which was in us, we watched the reeling masses, the agitated, limber schools of birds, scorched and delighted by the spectacle and, like someone over-wrought and up far too late—pulling out all the stops with a series of indecent flourishes, even those of sentimentality and relentlessness to suck, as if from a prawn's tiny claw, the meat of the music which nobody else wanted, hidden there—improvising on the manuals and pedals of the 64' pipe-organ perched aloft—like a starling on a miniature trapeze in a fretted stone cage with a bell to peck and its own looking glass—in some derelict suburban cathedral, relieved of the illusion that there is space and there is time.

And something deeply mawkish and phony in their place—the bell of the world as cracked as its mirror, with a ringing whine & a whistle, however gently it was clapped.

The ice on the sentimental lake was *thin!*

It was the starlings' task to teach us this. A frenzy—and almost real—yet the unreal *being* real too, because of these very cracks. Resembling theatre—the actors, in feigning character and emotion, true to themselves at last. Unless they fake feigning it.

Like when your bath overflows, and your bathmat is afloat, and you can see the floor tiles through hot water. But you can't get through the boiling flood to turn off the taps—or even to pull out the plug. You just close the bathroom door and possibly even the door to your flat and use will alone to make it stop. Prayer, that muscle of hope!

Noise, meanwhile, from the people downstairs—listeners you might call them—even commotion. What I mean is my spiritual machinery could not be governed and was overflowing. Some kind of overload in the aesthetic exultation circuits—crackling, distortion and feedback, whizz, hiss, hum—with, nevertheless, interesting transcendental corollaries. Judder, even. Which led on to a state of having been soothed—like a dog while you are stroking it—but soothed all through—in the mind too. Dualism was finished. Like pluralism. The one was one. As, it turned out, and not for the first time, it had *always* been. Overwhelmed, unable to cope, muddled, ultra-emotional, mentally garrulous, having blown something of a spiritual and above all aesthetic fuse, I closed my eyes. And felt something cold, burning, and wet on my hand—it was hers. But—

—I'm tired, she said abruptly, and flipped her face away as if I wanted to kiss her mouth. The starlings, though still visible performing their impossible manoeuvres above the distant port, had whirled into irrelevance. An ugly beauty—the ugliest bird with the ugliest song—perhaps the most human amongst the birds!—not even a screech—yet they manage to flock together to say something you could never have dreamt up yourself—like words.

Yet, too, I had the horrid knowledge that they were now fish and we were drowning. It's not that they looked like fish, they *were*—shining, reddish, finned with wings. It's not me, but the world that's crazy. And feathered. Besides, it quickly passed.

Time returned, but only to drag like a long engagement—but with, I hoped, a hidden wisdom, busy seasoning what might become our love. Whilst beneath us, climbing the same hill we in our gondola bounced and swang towards, was that counterbalance to our ancient cable-car, a miniature funicular—with its gushing, jetting and gurgling waters; its perching sprays of fern, straining to catch droplets on each drab yet luminous frond; its glazed brickwork and encaustic tiles; its trembling cars, in matchwood and wicker, dangling at the end of fraying cables on the steep inclined-plane. It was like being in a race to see who could go slowest. But as we watched it, the sky blackened again and our car made a vibrant, booming lurch. Her eyes opened, her lips opened, her teeth opened, and she gripped both my forearms and gasped. We had arrived! We'd won—or was it lost? And alighted, like visitors from the future, in the sky-port of the *Parc d'Atraccions* set as it was in the *Bosc Urbá.*

Here, a concrete platform was cantilevered over the city, dating from the time of the *Exposició Universal,* that visionary and joyous riposte of the nineteenth century to those drab Olympiads and monotonous *biennales* of the twentieth. Trade fairs, transposed into the domains of the body-athletic and of art.

The day was almost gone. Up here the failing sun still reached us, just, but had lost its verve. Down in the urban basin, under a layer of smog, night had fallen. And just as from the brake-lights of the cars, through all the chinks in the hardening crust of wall and roof and garden now shone an identical yellow light. The angled fabric below us was only a hollow city, masking subterranean fires. Only the fires were real.

—Have you brothers and sisters? she asked me as seated now we drank icy *San Miguel* and ate *picants.* How many? How old are they? Do you love them? Do you love your parents? Do you live altogether?
—I live with my girlfriend.

Her forehead pleated and she looked surprised. And then, after a long wait, her eyes glowing and distant, fixed on something near the ground:

—Is she lovely? I'll believe she is.

Next a trip on a Ferris wheel, and then on a wheel turned on its side—a spinning disc with a waxed parquet floor, around the rim of which we sat in monstrous tea-cups which, likewise, span horribly. Like life in this that, again and again, it all went wrong.

—This one, I don't like it at all, she shouted darkly and distinctly, moving over to the far side of the spinning tea-cup, as if I was crowding in on her.

So we chose to dodge the funhouse. It was packed and besides there was something formalistic about it, not sentimental enough, cold—the people wedged inside were screaming out of good form, not fear. It just didn't feel real. And as for the ghost train—where people really were screaming, but this time out of joy—fun though that was, as I pointed out to Ana, you could say that in some sense we were already on our own.

But that dance-floor with people waltzing—because at this I suppose the waxed parquet was meant to hint—we in our spinning tea-cups had been the pukka waltzing couples, whirling individually within the more stolid mass of the dance, itself revolving around an invisible drain. Not to mention that all this took place on a spinning landscape, itself revolving around a sun that had its own revolutionary agenda, with respect to our galaxy, the luminiferous aether, etc.. *And* the atoms of which the dancers, like vegetable portraits, green-men, were composed. We were in an infinite block of space, even without stirring from this place—perhaps the same went for time. Was I after all going mad? Impossible, if I already was? Yet, we never get the message the first time it whirls, so it has to whirl again.

—You know, I didn't like that one either, she'd repeated as we alighted and picked our way around a puddle of sick which had tumbled sparkling from above. The earth rolled like a barrel underneath our feet and I had to hold her up. I could feel her bones, under her clothes, and the place where her breasts erupted from her rib-cage.

—I would like to go now, she said, recoiling from my support and stumbling away with her arms outstretched like someone playing blind man's buff, in a wide reeling circle which brought her back to me.

An unauthorised dirt track led through a tear in the chain-link fencing at the back of the amusement park which, as we climbed the hill above it, shrank steadily until it was no bigger than a spotlit parking-lot.

Twisted Aleppo pines, as we walked, slid around us carnally, and in such a way that we seemed to be moon-walking on the edge of a revolving turntable, the nearer pines going backwards, the further forward, and somewhere, one tree or column or empty glade in the middle-distance acting as gnomon. The whole machine, local and universal, was driven by the impulse of our four tired feet.

—It's dark now, said Ana.
—What did you think?

It was past the hour at which I'd landed last night—the earth had spun once since the episode of the dog, and like a dial to indicate the passage of the year, inched a little further round the sun. Out from the druggy pines scrambled the path, then rose in zig-zags beneath cypresses, fenced by a cream-marble balustrade, the handrail of which was hollowed into a sloping gutter, darkened with algae. Black water sploshed into stone basins clogged with weeds, with indistinct, gleaming water-lilies and vague, bloated goldfish. Weaving under staggered arches, we climbed the hill of polished cobbles towards a crenellated silhouette. Amongst the successive pits and traps of the *glacis* of an old fortress, half-heartedly converted into a pleasure ground, was the anticlimax of a final grassy elevated platform, with backdrop of powdered stars. But with its baldness, came an exhilaration at steering, perhaps briefly, and only delusionally, this weird universe. With your hands (on its masses of galaxy and gas and other random curiosities) set at ten to three, a fuming fag dangling from the lax fingers with which you spin, whenever necessary, its great wheel. I.e. we were here, and had chosen to be.

Cats were growling and screeching under the fronds and spines of undergrowth which had reached that very shade where green may or may not be black.

Somewhere to one side we heard a scuffle and a small animal cried out.

Below us, but far away, and tilted slightly, on the opposite side of the sky from the stars, the darkening sea still glowed mildly with a distressed denim-blue. Above it, high intestinal clouds were tinted tangerine, yellow and peach by a sun which for us had set long ago.

—Sit down here, she said.

We watched the swirling afterbirth in the sky. Plus gross faces in the clouds—moon faces, stone faces, smiling, mad.

A jet was wheeling amongst them. No more than a chased silver reliquary with outstretched wings, each with the turned up wingtip of a paper dart, its torso pricked with glowing windows and pulsing lights, within which, pressed in mauve plush, I was shocked to see in a kind of a compulsory vision, that *I* lay, my feet together and my arms outstretched, my feet and hands curling and sweating with shame.

I asked myself—sentimentality, yes, I get that—but what's on the other side? Because, says Frost, *sometimes the best way out is through.* Maybe the remedy for sentimentality is not hot-footing it, like Flaubert or Joyce, into an emotionless portrayal of sentimentality, but using its own weight against it and penetrating to the domain of a *feeling* truth. It had to be worth a try.

The jet drifted down and, turning above the sea, dropped its wheels, spread its wings over the distant illuminated runway, lifted its beak and alighted with a whistle like a bird. The grating rumble of flight was replaced with the same frenetic but slowing cantering pulse, or else its illusion, when these wheels crossed the gaps between the enormous squares of pale concrete composing the runway, as a train makes crossing the joints between rails.

With a touch so hot I pulled away my fingers, she touched my hand.

—You know, I don't want to kiss you now, she warned me. Her face was blue and her hands were white, and the only points of light were in her teeth and in her eyes, reflecting the minute glare of the distant airport. She closed her lips, closed her eyes, widened her nostrils and breathed-in slowly, lowering her face, turning it from side to side, feeling the coldness of air through which came the hyper-real, miniaturised barking of dogs, protesting not against interlopers, but being itself.

She smelt of cooled skin, but peppered, burning in my nostrils and making my heart beat.

I touched her lips with my tongue and they opened, and when I touched her teeth she moved her face away suddenly, as if I had taken her lip between my teeth and bitten through. She struggled up and dusted the dead grass from her jeans.

—Tight-ass, I said in a spiteful but involuntary reprisal. I was hurt. But I'm ashamed—even now, shamed.
—What do you mean?
—Like sexy ...
—Oh.
—... only the reverse.
—Oh!
—No, but its sexy too, relenting.
—I want to go down now, she said.

The path curved through a bubbling waist-deep foam of creepers spiked with bluish clouds of thorn. Floating tendrils of bramble felt for our skin and tugged out drops of blood. Through a mask of dark trunks, the bright, matted city, stretched out beneath us, pulsed with the halting flow of lights in its veins.

—Oh! she said again, suddenly.
—What is it? I turned to her. All I could see was the faint shape of her face within her hair, and her hands hanging neatly by her side.
—I'm tired. And scared, she said, her voice addled with doom. I can feel my tired leg-bone inside my leg. And I have blisters.
—It isn't far, don't worry.
—Oh no, it's alright to worry. It was all waste of time. Waste of time. All of it.
—When we get to the bottom, I'll buy you another *San Miguel*.
—*If* .... she corrected in a gloomy voice. *If* we get there.

But a little later I heard her laughing as we scrambled through the brambles and the razor grass.

—What?
—And a dish of almonds!
—And a dish of almonds.
—Don't leave me.

—Of course I won't leave you. I sounded cross.
—Ever?

The word, in her flat breathy voice, made me stop, and then turn back to her. I couldn't see her face now.

—I don't know.
—You know, I was only joking, she said in a serious way.

She kept quiet after that. I took her hand and wove my fingers through it. At first her hand was limp. But then she squeezed, seemed to think a while, and pressed her lips against my knuckles and held them there. We'd come, at last, out of the plunging, tangled *matas* into one of those districts where the streets are lit ultra-dimly, with an occasional brighter pond of light, and are packed with milling beggars as if for the curtain-up of an *operetta*. Wild palms and figs sprouted between the kerb-stones, displacing them. Awaiting the overture's end before starting her song, a mother with a grubby face was seated on the pavement under a street-lamp brighter than the rest, the baby in her lap looking up in astonishment as if her face was the sky and her eyes were planets. Dirty cats ranged around her, glossy bunches of fruit-like excrement steamed on cobbles, and semi-retired tarts, baked in make-up, plus pregnant, childish ones, strutted unconvincingly in arcs and figures of eight behind.

—Tricky place, said Ana, and drew away from me as if it was my fault. She was tired under her brittle skin and in the light of these streets her colours had run. Her eyes were pink as well as blue, her lips were blue as well as pink.

—Tricky, not a good place to come, she added. We go, quick!

The pinkish blue in her eyes turned a denser, more stupid colour, and her lower lip stuck out. Something was wrong. When I thought of kissing her, I felt sick.

Two handsome Africans barged past and made us stumble and we saw the rising yellow moon, the moon of the night of the dog, blocking our way at the end of the street, and heard shouted warnings as one man battered the breast of another with the blade of a jack-knife, but slowing as we watched, slower, deeper, with a grainy sigh, almost on the edge of stopping, as if at the stringy heart of the district time itself was running out. Ana suddenly lifted my arm around her shoulders and by clinging made it hard to walk. I sucked-in the sugary air from her scalp. She was stuttering.

—Are you angry? she asked.
—No!
—No, angry, *angry!* She still stuttered, but there were glittering facets in her eyes.
—Hungry?
—Yes, angry.
—Yes.

Four balding palms had been poked into the sand of her square and a dry fountain in the middle overflowed with torn black-plastic sacks and their innards of yellowed newspaper and tins. Hanging low above us, the massive stonework of her apartment building was strutted and punctured like a magnified skull, strung with balconies of cast-iron shrubbery and brambly railing, all turning brown in a chemical autumn and falling in showers of rust.

Inside, the staircase lurched around the edges of a stairwell which disappeared into darkness both up and down. It had the air not of having been built but hollowed. On each floor as we climbed was a faint, whirring gaslight, revealing doors cluttered with verdigris and porcelain—handles in the form of hands, doorbells shaped like insects and glass spy-holes with lashed rims in the shape of eyes. Stained-glass windows, cracked but mended with scorched tape, gave onto a light-well so like a well that you imagined water reflecting the sky from its foot. More ferns grew from cracks in its glazed white bricks.

—The children *plays* with balls and breaks the window, she said.

Each floor was so similar to the last that as we climbed doggedly upwards it took an effort of will to believe we had moved at all. We were marching in place. And yet the numbers stencilled on the plaster flipped and the banister, starting as tangled creepers, died slowly back to nothing but a thin steel band. Hers was the only door at the end of the highest flight.

On it, a small brass label-holder, and her name—*Ana Catta*—written in that beautiful schoolroom script, with its slow enormous curves and tilts, its serif-like hooks, of the semi-literate, presumably her landlord or the building's janitor.

As she unlocked it, she looked away from me.

—'Before I came to it, my apartment was for lift machinery,' she said, 'but they took away the lift. I got it together for myself—whitewash it and use larch boards to block up the lift-well under the table.'

They sagged when you stepped on them.

—'Have you ever had anyone to supper before,' I asked. There was a long pause, then—

—'No,' she said. 'But I can lift up a board and drop coins down it just for the sound. We could do it after if you like. I drop empty bottles down and listen for the smash.'

Something about the silence as they fell as different from most silence—a silence not so much of screaming as of waiting, of patience—but then *we're* not the bottle. Perhaps it's like that sorry 'joke' about someone, falling, passing the first floor and saying *so far so good*. And I thought of Alice, falling—and having time to rearrange the cupboards on the walls of the rabbit-hole on the way down. What is it with this nonsense stuff—why not just be sensible like everyone else?

Then—a distant grateful smash like the sound of the dustbin-people in the dawn—the broken bottle returns to its own on a tower of splintered glass. Would this tower ever tap the underside of her thin larch boards?

When they took out the lift they'd not removed all the lift-machinery—some of it had been been too big to shift. Stand up too suddenly from the table on its yielding larch boards and you banged your head on the cable drum, inside which she stored her fleecy jumpers and spare jeans. I could see that to get into the bedroom, which was where, raised on cast-iron stumps above her mattress, the lift-motor, like a late Paolozzi, brooded on its lost yet exciting past, you had to crawl under the crank-spindle. Great toothy gear-wheels of selected diameters, supported on exuberant, flowing, cast-iron brackets and bearings, still engaged and turned in different senses when the clutch was disengaged. It was now us, shrunk to flea-size, who flitted & played amongst the pulsing innards of a transparent watch. I suppose we were its hands, if not the numbers on its face—i.e. an outcome and not a cause of the revolutions of this vintage machine. A repercussion, perhaps. We didn't drive it, it drove us. Yet, like those birds that nest in the innards of a machine, she'd stopped it running. Like, even, those stowaways in the wheel-arches of aeroplanes.

Cats who sleep in car-engines, toddlers playing hide-and-seek in fridges and tumble-dryers. The litter of puppies under the steam-hammer, the dog beneath the wheel. The spirit of the dump, of counting to a hundred, of recolonising the landfill with its wheedling gulls—and the grumble of the diggers busy covering it all up, sextons of excess, and therefore of life itself.

Her walls were concrete, webbed with cracks. Electric wiring was nailed across the surface and pinned on one wall there was a municipal poster advertising last year's *Rua de la Disbauxa* and *Rua de l'Extermini*, with one corner dangling over like the folded ear of a dog. The plywood table—lodged above the lift-well and beneath the cable-drum—was covered with a plastic oil-cloth with a sprigged flower pattern, pinned around the edges with rusty drawing pins.

On a shelf frilled the same sprigged-flower oil-cloth, she kept her modest collection of snow-domes, including one of the famous, molten cathedral whose termite spires were visible from all over this city. She shook them for me one by one, explaining their virtues. Absurd to hoard snow-domes in this southern city. Yet it did snow here, she promised me, the roof outside her apartment was sometimes turfed with snow, and the statues in a row along the parapet wore comical white berets, like a Rembrandt negative from behind.

Then, leaving me gazing, head tilted, at the blizzards inside, she unplugged the butane canister from the *Super Ser* stove in her bedroom and rolled it on its rim into the box-like kitchen where she attached it to the cooker's gas nozzle. Detaching myself like a hypnotist's subject from the soothing domes, and rattling open a flimsy glass door, I went out onto the terrace to see the statues. There was a wind moving a faint cold smog in from the harbour and the air smelt of diesel and fish.

The lift-machinery flat had been built on the roof of the apartment block, and I could walk right round it, behind the backs of the statues lining the façades. On one the sculptor, macabre and wry, had represented the exposed vertebrae, the branching trachea, and all the tangled, worm-like tubes of the sitter's guts.

Through the lighted window of the kitchen, which resembled the window of an isolated shack, lost deep in an urban wilderness, I could see Ana chopping a salad of carrots, beetroots and olives with fast efficiency. She opened a tin of tuna. And, as a saucepan of water began to blister, slit a foil-packet of soup-powder and stirred it in. Taking a wooden spoonful of soup, she blew on it and lowered her lips onto it, cautiously, to taste.

—Already ready, she sang out, and I came back in. As we sat down, the larch boards bowing beneath us, she was a little out of breath and trying not to smile. But as she ate, she couldn't help looking distinctly victorious and each time she opened her mouth to put some salad in, of its own accord it smiled. Beetroot stained the centre of her lips black.

—More salad? she asked when I had finished the mound on my plate.
—I couldn't if you paid me, I said.

She gave me more. Love, babies just epiphenomena—the meaning of life being food.

When she'd finished both her salad and her soup, she picked up a wine-glass with both hands, like a child, which made it look too big for her. I heard her swallow.

Our knees touched underneath the table and she drew her knee away, but then it came back again, gently. We ate some hard damp cheese with quince jelly. It tasted nothing like dog and I felt I'd come out the other end of *that*. She wasn't talkative, and when she did talk she had a serious, almost earnest face. Then she laughed without any warning and her looks changed instantly—hungry, daring, showing her teeth and leaning out towards you as if she wanted to wrap you in her legs and even kiss you. And then her eyes flamed up, and she thought of something which made her pause and flush and hold her glass to her cheeks to cool them.

—I drink all the wine, she said. You drink some. And although I had mine, and it was full, she offered me her own glass, making a face whose sparking allure amounted to a command. I drank.

Her hair, which had resumed its corkscrews as the day wore on, had now gone limp and feathery, since the unvented butane-stove was burning, lacing the air with water vapour amongst other things, so that in profile the line from her nose to the top of her head was one smooth turning curve.

Having eaten, she was determined we should play cards. I had no chance to resist as, breathing deeply, her cheeks still flushed, she drew elaborate grids and boxes on a spring-bound pad to tally the score.

—He plays like this, she said, in the soothing, automatic tones always used for explaining rules to madmen.

Again, something deeply carnal about the marching-in-place of a card game, like somebody giving head with ice cubes in their mouth. I won several games in a row, only by chance because it was a game of chance, and the fact that I won pleased her, as being a credit to her teaching and her discrimination.

—You've played before! she told me, staring into my eyes with a burning, brimming smile which rushed time itself.

She was squeezing my ankles in hers as we played, but you wouldn't have known it by the thoughtful look on her face as she valued the assets in her hand and moving her lips as she did so, chose which to give up. Once, her face seemed to swell with excitement.

—Now I shall win *you* this time at last! she said, fanning out her cards in a rigid curve like the tail of a dove and looking at me feverishly over their backs. But it turned out, as she lay her hand face-up on the table, that she had mistaken the queen of clubs for the queen of spades.

—Oh! she said, petulantly. Boring game. We'll play a different game.

Before I answered she flushed pale red, looked up at me in confusion, and began to stutter.

—What? I asked her.
—You like music? she said.
—What sort of music.
—*Velvet Underground?*
—Is that it?
—Yes, she said, as if it was a silly question. Or *Nico?*
—I'm game.
—No game.
—No, *game.*
—What signifies *game?*
—It means *yes.*

I steered the butane stove back into her bedroom, where the music was, and waited on the edge of her bed, which was a narrow mattress on the floor, while she went to boil us tea. With it she brought a two-litre bottle of cooking sherry, squeezed into an armpit whose shoulder, by slipping out, it shrugged.

—*Ai-ai-ai-ai-ai,* she was calling in alarm, and I rescued it just as the bottle began to accelerate.

—Sugar? she asked.
—No, thanks.

Ana took sugar, several spoons of it, straight into her mouth. Her face took on briefly a furtive look. Her *Bush* hi-fi: speaker, amp, turntable were in one lidded box, veneered in black leatherette so that it had not only the voice of life but its skin. The fascia glowed when she switched it on, fired as it was by hell, aka the infernal combustion of coal-fired power stations. In it she stacked her two albums on a cranked spindle to drop to the black felt turntable one by one, before sitting back with a face of intelligent satisfaction to listen.

The tea she'd made was from chopped, dried mint. She didn't have a strainer. In the cups the fragments of mint whirled like birds in a storm in a wood.

And then, whilst still revolving, settling. Which clarified what had bothered me about the starlings earlier. If in their flocking they were being sentimental, gushing—this was like a Venn diagram—they were also being staggering, shocking—the riposte in another medium, because their own literal music as starlings was to our senses so ugly, to Vivaldi or Pachebel. But where was the stone of which they were the flesh—that stone with the germ of the future? The stone had been the dangling gondola and the germ was Ana and me. Around this, nothing was fixed, everything was in motion in relation to itself, but we, at the centre, had been breathless, still. And yet, still, the ice on the sentimental lake was *thin!*

Her solid, blunt, painful boots, cut in black leather, were crossed at the ankles.

—I like them, I told her.

Neat as hoofs, too big for her, yet winning. She looked embarrassed, but I'd said the right thing.

—I bought them yesterday, before I came out to see the *corrida de toros* where I saw you.

Later she had me pull them off, and we sat in a state of pleasing innocence, she with her leg tucked now so that the wrinkled heel of her sock, stained pale brown by boot-lining, was wedged against her thigh right at the top. The easiness with which she chattered and laughed, shook out the damp, dark flames of her hair and made fun of me was something clean and hot, a first meal at home after a difficult trip—and a welcome bath.

—Take something now? she asked politely, pouring us each a sherry the colour of brown sugar in a tumbler moulded, in brittle fairground glass, in the shape of a bunch of grapes. Her white jeans had folded into symmetrical waves along her legs, except where taut across her knees and sprung in her hollow lap. Between the jeans and her socks was a stretch of pale leg, narrow about the ankle and just swelling into calf, where fine gold hairs grew. The heat of the stove or of the sherry had printed dull pink patches at the top of her cheeks, which pressed up against her eyes giving them the squeezed, glandular look of a squirrel.

—Are you hot? she asked me, and folding her arms she pulled her fluffy turtle-jersey over her head.

She made the waves of her ringleted fringe float in her own breath and pumped at the belly of her shirt to cool her breasts. She was wearing a man's white shirt, open at the neck to show a small gold figure dying in agony on its cross, and she had a habit of sucking this so the gold chain came out at either end of her lips like a snaffle. Folding carefully first on one side and then the other she turned up her sleeves beyond the elbow. Then, with an air of not knowing what to do next, she took another sip of sherry and blushed. She was panting.

—It's too hot, she said, and the cross, still in her mouth, clinked.
—Take off your shirt?

She was uncertain whether to be offended or amused, but something inevitable in the idea got a grip on her. After a while she began smiling like a witch, then very slowly, button by button, looking down as she did so with concern, as if her breasts were being blown up with a bicycle pump, she undid it.

—There, she said, tugging the ends out of her trousers and resting her hands on her folded knees. The shirt was open a little, so that I could see the edges of her breasts and her narrow, hard belly, swelling on the waist of her jeans. Then she hugged the opened shirt around her. Her eyes had a stirred up, turbid look which bypassed me.

—I am such fool, she said sullenly Always the same again!

And she reached out behind her for the sherry glass.

She didn't want to take her trousers off. But she wanted to drink the sherry, and when she had done so she wanted to take her trousers off. She didn't though: she felt too shy. Instead she looked at me softly, her resonant eyes squinting slightly and watering with alcohol.

—That you have more drink, she instructed me, and as she leant across to fill up my glass, her shirt fell open and she ran her nipple slowly down my arm, which felt it could slice my skin. There was an innocent catch in her breath. She was looking very serious, and somewhat stupid, but heroic and stirring. She had the thing of making your eyes go out of focus when you looked at her, and brim with tears.

—I am *stupid!*, she confirmed. And she laughed, joyful.

She hadn't let go of the bottle, which she was gripping hard by the throat while she picked carefully at the label, and having finished off her tumbler, and filled mine again, she held the bottle up in two hands and glugged some sherry down. A viscous braid of it dripped from her chin to her belly. She was becoming sleepy and affectionate, and kept holding my eyes now in a radiant, ill-defined stare.

—Want more? she asked, holding out the bottle with her eyebrows raised. I drank more. Quite naturally, as I did so, she knelt on the bed with her ear pressed into the mattress, unzipped her jeans and slid them and her knickers slowly and clumsily over her hips and down her thighs. When they reached her knees she fell sideways and tried to work them over her feet.

Her skin cold and white, and damp, as if the moisture from the butane stove had condensed not just on the walls, but on her body.

—I'm sleeping now, she announced. But she had got in a tangle with her feet: the jeans came inside out, seeming to wear the underpants on the outside like *Superwoman* does, and they wouldn't come over her heels. Eventually she gave up struggling and went limp.

I fed my hands up inside the empty legs and caught hold of her feet which began wriggling, and she laughed and rolled around. I got her trousers off for her, and still wearing her open shirt and her stained ankle socks, she lifted the covers of the bed and slid her two legs down through the damp sheets, looking intently at her hands holding the bedspread and clinking the crucifix against her teeth as she sucked. Now she squinted at me.

—It's too late to go to the hotel. Sleep here if you like to, she said, taking the cross from her mouth and holding it in front of her moving lips as she spoke.
—I'm game, I said. And she laughed happily.
—Game! she said.

I took off my shirt and then my shoes and kneeled on the narrow mattress beside her. But she lay her hand in the way, palm up, and wouldn't let me lie down.

—No, she said, keeling over slightly.
—Why not?

She giggled vaguely, her head unsteady on her neck, and pointing at my flies burst into artificial laughter as if I had done something hilarious.

—Forgot to take trousers off.

—Ok, she said, now I turn out the light.

She leant deliberately across me, scoring my cheek with one breast.

—Sleep well, I heard her whisper to herself.

—I'm game, she whispered, and giggled.

The day had been hot, in the sun at least. The night was cold. The butane stove was burning with a guttural whirring and threw a bluish-orange light on our faces. The walls wept with condensation. Ana turned away as if she meant to sleep, but her cold flesh pressed suddenly on my hip bone, opened and engulfed it, and I felt a lubricated heat.

I rested against her back and held her breasts. Time passed. Her breathing softened. I thought she was asleep until she whispered something and felt back between her legs, tugging at me.

—Ana?

She didn't answer, but let go.

Yet, after a sulky pause, her bottom began to rotate ultra-slow. My breath was going quickly and my mind went hot and dim, as if I was blowing up a *Lilo.* But then she pulled away petulantly and propped herself on unsteady pillows. By the light of the burning butane, her hair covered her face in a matted curtain which she lifted with one hand to try to drain the empty sherry glass. She wanted sex, but wanted sherry more.

She found the bottle somehow, and topped us both up. Then she wanted to put her legs and arms around me, and slid down the bed and rolled me until I lay between her bent legs, on top of her. Her thighs squeezed me harshly. She wanted our bodies to fuse.

—Ana, are you drunk?

She had her eyes shut, and her head was forced crookedly into the crack between the pillow and the mattress. She screwed up her face and arched her back and her lips drew down at the ends and came open over her even, off-white teeth and she twisted and tried to push me away with her hands. But the insides of her thighs were gripping my hips so hard that I felt our bones grate.

Pinned underneath me, translucent belly upwards, like a glass-backed watch whose insides you can see, her arms pushing me away and her neck doubled back, the light of the butane stove showed her voice box sliding up and down inside her throat like a lift, and the hollow frog of her chin, and the upper horseshoe of teeth enclosing her shadowed, fishbone palate. She began to move her legs in the prudish yet immodest gestures of the breast-stroke and made a crying noise, which made me come.

We didn't move after that, but lay tangled in each other with the butane whirring in the stuffy orange night, already asleep.

Far ahead surf was beating on a long, low cliff, which came no closer as I slid down the side of each wave, throwing up a burbling wash. The dog, the self-same dog, who had been gambolling ahead of me, fell into difficulties. First his paws and then more and more of his body was sinking. He was having to make violent, laborious bounds across the surface of the water, panting doggy-style through black lips. As I overtook, he fell behind.

A sudden, choppy, cross-swell, with a click swallowed the dog, who I could now see, his eyes open and his fur and cheeks undulating, swimming along beneath me. Elongated bubbles slipped out through gaps in his teeth. The green water turned blue, then battle-ship grey, and with the sound of handfuls of gravel thrown in, it started to rain.

It was only Ana, closing the drapes with a wave-like gesture to keep out the light. She was naked and as she moved she leaned forwards from her pelvis as if her breasts were over-ripe—the trunk of her body steady and firm, her belly sucked in, her lobed behind pressed out. She had the scary elegance of a beast.

When with a glimpse at me she saw my eyes half open, she paused and turned towards the bed. Her arms were dangling by her sides, knuckles forwards, and she was slightly stooped. With short, tuneful yelp of joy she leapt, and landed straddling me on all fours. I had closed my eyes by reflex, but I could hear breathing as she studied my face. I felt her face brought closer, and high up on my forehead, near the hair, a kiss. More breathing. Studying my face again. Another kiss.

With the same, wave-like gesture she flapped open the bedclothes, manoeuvred underneath, and flopped them back over her. She was straddling me again, and her cold skin, where it touched mine, did not yield. Holding herself up on her arms like a mermaid she swung her hair across my face, her breasts across my chest, and she moved her pelvis slightly. The effect was to stroke the flat place between her legs against my abdomen. There was something wet and gentle in her face. She was out of breath.

—Kinky.
—Kinky?
—Like tight-ass.
—Oh! she said.
—Only the reverse.
—Are you lying me again?

Distrust masked a sweet elation.

—No.
—Here, she said in a husky voice, wiping her lips before bringing them in close. Her face was having the same effect on me as alcohol. You know, I think I like you very much, she added, and gasped.

Her movements, which had been fluid, became savage. I saw different parts of her body, her stomach, her breasts, dangling from the branches of her ribs, her thighs, her waist. Her breathing, too, was jerky. And yet the texture of the skin between her legs which had been bristly and coarse was now oiled and soft.

—Ana, I whispered, and froze.
—Yes? she asked in a doubtful voice, withdrawing herself from me, but I was only saying her name. It made her moan.

She had lowered her chest onto mine, turning her face to the side and resting it on my face, and she reached back her hands as if to sit on them, making a rearrangement between her legs which allowed her body to sink very slowly back onto mine. She seemed to have fallen asleep, until she lifted herself up on her arms, stricken by an unexpected doubt, and examined my face. Suddenly I could see through her transparent eyes, felt I was falling, and grasped at the twisted sheets to either side of me.

—I love you, I said. But my voice cracked as I spoke, and went up a register, so I sounded like Minnie Mouse.

But now she was almost choking, resting her open mouth on my open mouth, sucking in the air which came from my lungs, moaning still more. I could feel the weight of the flesh coating her weightless bones.

She had an ugly expression on her lips, but her moaning had the purity of tone and monotony of pitch of a tuning fork. I could feel its hypnotic and delicious resonance between my eyes. The butane whirred more loudly, singing-along. The noise was that of a fly on a window. And her movements were in slo-mo, and she wanted to nestle her face beside my neck. And in the end she wasn't moving at all. Her body became soft, and moulded on mine.

We shifted slightly, somehow absent from our minds.

Her saliva had the after-taste of sugar.

Perhaps with a little egg.

On her back now, her knees were cocked apart and I lay between them, and the idea, when it struck me, of how I was lying on her naked skin between her open legs was as intoxicating as reality itself. I closed my eyes. My scrotum was squeezed firmly, as in a man's fist, but also gently, in a way which gave me grounds for profound satisfaction. And my belly began to move like a mechanical toy, as regularly as breathing in and out.

But as I moved, a quarry or strip-mine unfurled to either side of me, barren of plants. They seemed to be mining a powdery, bone-white dust. I saw this through the closed lids of my eyes. Meanwhile the movement in my belly went on without any effort of will, relentless, shaming, as pneumatic not as breath, but as a drill.

My member bruised and sore.

A dumb-bell shaped, copper-green pool, at the lowest point in the quarry which, though awake, I could see clearly through closed eyes, gurgled with enigma, and sank into un-wetted dust.

And then I saw—there was no option not to—the copper-green pool reconstituted, between the green razor-leaves of a few palm-like plants which had just sprouted around it. Before it gurgled and sank again into powder.

But the movement went on, involuntary, painful, grinding, dull. A ruthless bouncing on her pale, spread body, with all the blood drained from it, nailed not to a cross but a mattress. Her vinegary saliva, her pierced side.

Kissing her lips I felt I was suffocating, that her lips would never be withdrawn from mine. I turned my face far away to grope for breath. I inhaled deeply, without refreshment. The air smelt faintly, of indole and stale cigarette. Our sexual organs made a farting sound as I withdrew. I made it to the window and opened it.

Through a wormhole in the blowing sea-fog in which the night had earlier submerged the city, you could hear the shrieking of the cable-car's great yellow wheel—pierced as it was with circles of varying sizes, and smeared with dabs and chunks of a glass-like lubricant in which trapped feathers no doubt vibrated still—down preened from the breasts of the pigeons which nested there. There was a mystical charge of some sort, an immanence, to the noise of this wheel which manifested itself as the wheel, though still revolving, also ceasing to revolve, which perhaps meant only that I was now revolving too. And this revolutionary stillness seemed to extend or unfurl like a wing our own cramped world into a parallel, invisible dimension for the purpose of milling or grinding something, maybe bone, maybe powdered eye.

You could hear, as well, the hiss then thud of the pile-driver extending the mole, and the clank of the ships in the harbour, whose fresh scent, of diesel and fish, you could smell. You could smell, too, a doggy scent on the wind. Whirling, rocking, whacking, swinging and stillness—it seemed these were the only movements allowed, and each had its own meaning or corresponding category of being, distinct not only in its mode of movement but its wide requirements of the world. All other movements (the nested counter-whirling of the amusement park tea-cups! Retching!) were simply composed of these. And all this—though it should have been no worse than musing in a rocking chair on a jiving planet—yet it was!

The fog was getting everywhere, even into my lungs, and my ears, and of course my mind, and it turned her loveable, hidden shanty, hanging above the stirring city, into the gondola of a gratifyingly fireproof airship, whose gutta-percha envelope was cloud.

The fog hid much but what it disclosed was not only noise but the pressing conviction (I have to own it, however shamefully comic—because it was one of the principal fruits of that long night) that we were living inside a vast dog—call it the *Trojan Dog*. Or—I had to challenge such flamboyant excess—the question had come up again—was I just mad? If mad, at least I wanted to be honest. Because there's overlap.

Now an unexpected fog-rent opened to display a disk of blue sky transfixed by the course of a jewelled and howling airliner. We could hear, too, a siren, a would-be saxophonist, the carnal slap of waves on the harbourfront. And even, sometimes, squidged and even inverted by time and distance, the colourful, tinny, remorseless music-and-screams of the *Parc d'Atraccions*, tilted invisibly at its rakish angle, up on its hill. Plus a cockerel and a gull. Whilst far beneath us, in one of the apartments of her block, through a window giving onto the glazed-brick light-well, someone was still practicing that provoking passage in a *fugue*, making the ferns vibrate and making, each time, however long the run-up, the same mistake, so that as Ana had pointed out through salad, the evening before, it was not the *fugue* they were practicing at all, but the mistake. While from another flat came masculine screeching, and all of these sounds were subsumed, bound, lacquered, homogenised by fog into another modern composition, figurative yet abstract, poly-stylistic and, like the one I'd heard in the cab, in *faithfully* depicting it, more modern than modern life itself.

Yet, when Ana called to me from where she lay on her back, all the sounds stopped. The whirring butane cut in again. Her face turned to the ceiling, her arms outstretched, her skin bluish in the white light like someone whose operation didn't come off. Her voice was muffled and I couldn't understand what she said. She spoke again but I still couldn't hear. She was biting her lips.

I came back to lie on her body, which had the smooth, matte texture of cheese, but with uncomfortable lumps where her bones pushed up like tent poles against stretched fields of skin, and was flattened against the ruched bunches, rhythmic as music, of the crumpled sheet. Her chin was turned awkwardly to the side and down.

While she lay still, I slid inside of her and began to move. And looking into those sorry eyes, semi-opaque again, I lost my moral balance, as if someone lifted the side of the mattress to tip us off, and I wrapped my hands in the bundles of sheet on either side of her head. She turned her face to look at me. Her lips were pursed. Her eyes were wet, her deep eye sockets, as she lay on her back beneath me, filling slowly with tears which had nowhere to run. They smelt of sea-water, boiled, and trembled with our motion.

Her sweaty face, just below mine, sank onto her skull and was beginning to lose its definition as if time itself was going too fast. Her nearly lifeless eyes the only remaining life in a mask-like face, yielding, and miserable. As I looked she retreated even from these, and her body was limp and bouncing under my restless movement—eternal as the strokes of that glossy personage whose job it is to bang with lurid gestures, by flame-light, with the thigh bone of an ancestor, the very biggest gong at the vintage movie's start.

She might have been the body of a *dead* girl.

I found myself, in that half-delirious state that comes before sleep, estimating the bill at my hotel.

I remembered the dog. I saw the hairs of his throat creep as, lying in the road, he swallowed, rearranging, like a cravat, the folds in his neck. And suddenly coiling out of him, apparently independently of the rolling wheel, came the crimped pink bundle of inner-tubes, bile and plasma. He had looked angry before the tyre went over him, but afterwards peeved.

Ana's knees, which had cocked themselves on either side of my hips, slipped downwards again until her legs were lying flat on the sheets. My hands, which I discovered had been gripping her arm muscles, slid out along her outstretched arms until they were gripping her wrists. And, in a reflex to the pressure on her tendons, her hands furled into claws.

Her lips were tinted blue, and when her eyes, which had closed, began to partially re-open, her pupils were large. One eye hardly opened at all, but the gaze in the other swung aimlessly about.

The movements of her throat and of her eye were the only movements she made. When she swallowed the struts of the tendons in her neck and the horizontal rings of her windpipe moved under the skin. Tired creases ran around her neck. Her lips were expressionless, slightly compressed. Another swallow.

I released her wrists and her hands opened. Her arms rested where they were, outspread. My hands were moving down her body, the fingers and thumbs of each hand almost meeting around her waist and sliding on over her rocky hips. The will of someone to be born battered my belly on her white abdomen, stiff and grimy as a swan's wing swatting on water to scare you or even to take off, in a spume of downy feathers which floated more slowly down around us than soap suds, revolving like the fixed stars, while underneath her back the springs in her mattress moaned like ropes.

In my mind I could step away and walk about the room, inspecting snow domes and the view from the window—a view of fog.

Perhaps a pillow or a quilt had burst. The constellations of feathers drifted around us in bunched and shifting galaxies, but really like snow when not set on falling but just flurrying slowly, giving you the impression that you yourself are spinning on your own axis, while also orbiting solemn around a fixed point. Yet this was the feathers, not you.

Your movement was of a quite different sort—the rocker of an oil-well grunting out its own take on silencing the music of the spheres.

Anyhow, what the feathers disclosed, which bare space could not have done, is that we were swirling helplessly (with a synced inflation and collapse, but in a misshapen way) and as if there were no such thing as a wishing not to. But now all the feathers, spell broken, had fallen suddenly to the floor, which in the colourless light appeared, as a result. to be covered with frozen glass.

The cold cheeks of her bottom, to the eye no bigger than a large cotton handkerchief, felt ballooning to the touch. My hands found the crack dividing these and followed it as a pilot a gleaming railway, until they reached her puckered anus. Pressing against it with my fingertips, sinking a little, and turning this key in a stiff and rusted lock brought me to a climax with no edge to it, hardly noticeable, a climax perceptible more in the slowing down of my movements than anything else, and in a dribble of spunk.

A sensitivity amounting to pain, yet related closely to ticklishness, in the helmet of my cock froze me where I was just as tellingly as volcanic mud, hardening to tufa, froze the copulating couples of Pompeii.

Closing my teeth, I drew it out. It had blood on it. A flash of chafed skin, coated with slime, lips swollen and red as the lips of a toothless man. As I watched he seemed to gibber a few words and dribble something out.

—You know, I hate you, I think, I heard Ana say, but faintly, from a distant room, and looked up to see a sullen, angry face, still wet around the eyes with tears.

She drew her lips back from her teeth and sucked in the air. Then she shrieked unexpectedly, flipping her head from side to side and breathing too quickly and too deep, until one of her flapping hands caught the side of my nose, filling my throat with the bitter smell of bruised gristle. Then blood ran down from one of my nostrils and dripped on her face. Only by reflex, I raised my hand. She became limp, tranquillised, and only the crescent-shaped lumps at the ends of her lips still taut.

—I hate you, I think, she whispered again.

Her face was plain. Apart from the colour, which had already run, much of her beauty had been in the tension between the shape of her eyes and the shape of her lips. Her lower lip was now pressed up towards her nose and her chin was dented with pox-like depressions. Her nostrils flared and her skin went red. Her eyes shut.

I felt like getting up.

—What is it Ana? I asked, bent double on the edge of the bed and tying my shoe-laces.
—You know what is it, she said, in a low tremolo.

—Go away, she added. Far away.

Then something went down the wrong way, and she coughed until breathless.

—Quickly, she shouted through coughs, and paused to gasp, trying to calm herself. She was finding it hard. Now!, she gasped.

Her body had shrunk on her bones. A small trail of snot hung from her nostril. She seemed to be worsening, coughing desperately, and turning blank eyes towards me, set in a reddening face.

I too wanted to go. But feeble, misguided chivalry kept me back until with a long, slow, breath which sounded like a siren starting up, she tightened her naked belly and seemed to gather all her ribs like a necklace up around her neck, screwing up her face and screaming, as loudly as anyone can. She only stopped when the choking began again.

Closing the door of her flat, in the darkness of her hall I heard a whooping and cackling that bubbled up from nowhere and made me sweat and crouch. It was *me*, laughing the way you laugh at a car-smash, especially when *you* were driving and, the only one to have survived, are deciding where to have lunch. God exists, she is the devil, so to speak. Or— a lion in the city! Behind the door, above the laughter, Ana cried out in a singed pain with an underlying ground of revulsion.

But I couldn't stop. I'd got the cackles, of a sort which feel as if, illegally squatting your body, someone has requisitioned your lungs, your cheeks, your eyes. Giving rise to a tacky shame which won't wash off, especially from the place in your forehead between where the horns would sprout, plus a wet patch between your shoulder-blades where the wings might. In a brief gap in both the choking and cackling, when we both held our breath to listen, through the flimsy door, hollow as a guitar, I heard the sound of a match strike. It is maybe what Bellow calls the ordeal of desire: it's not that we want to possess what we desire, it's that we want by possessing it to be released from the desire. So, the striking of a match, unless it was just the scrape of a ply table shoved off thin larch boards.

Later, as I rode past on the way to the airport, scanning the road carefully, I glimpsed on the other carriageway the oily, dog-shaped cardboard cut-out, glued to the blacktop, which all that was left of the dog.

I saw him sitting again to rest, panting quickly, his tongue out, very upright and proper, a dog god, his tail laid neatly around his feet to warm them. He was like someone you see on a beach knocked down by a breaker and laughing, knocked down by a second and gasping, knocked down by a third and glugging for help.

—*No se puede devolver el dentífrico al tubo,* was roughly what that earlier driver had told me, or so I thought. Meaning you can't unring a bell, or even avoid salivating. But perhaps he had said something quite different. I was left, though, with the image of a silver tube of reddish, whitish oil-paint, rolled up to extrude the the last few globs of mysterious and universal colour, snaking and twirling out, pink as a kiss, orange as the sun, black as death, from the shadows inside the tube where it had not been colour at all.

At check-in, since we were to be late taking off on account of the fog, we got enormous mauve & green raffle-tickets. The tickets allowed us to join a queue for sandwiches with perspiring cheese, and abnormally small bottles of warmish *San Miguel*—the tickets larger than the bottles. Which led me, predictably, via cheese, as ever, back to dog.

A fellow traveller—I knew him from somewhere, just couldn't say where—tore his tickets into mauve and green confetti, scattered it in the air and then, as it glittered and spangled down, stamped it vainly into the floor—in fact perhaps he wasn't stamping-in at all, just jiving. The *biros* came out of his breast-pocket; blue, black, red—cold shades; and a silver wing of hair flopped across his forehead. His steel-rimmed glasses came off and tinkled on polished marble. Was it something to do with marriage? With the symbolisation of marriage? That garden of dead flowers, with its crisp & slowly revolving showers of petal?

Some crackly old films, after a customary banging of the gong, begin with the titles written in scraps of paper which then blow away. My mind kept wandering. I could bring it back, but it took duress.

And as, at last!, the carcass of the screeching, stinking jet accelerated along the runway, eager to fake by means of those engines, dangling and heavy as testicles, the necessary lightness to ascend, a phrase got stuck in my head like a song, inexplicably scary, whether true or false. I was unable to dislodge it, even with *Tainted Love,* that faithful resource of the mesmerised. It went: *You are the dog. You are the dog.*

To Milk a Unicorn

> A lovely woman, yes, clothed in delight,
> Is a generous feast where many can suck,
> An endless spring, yes,
> But of milk.
> (Lohenstein, *Agrippina.*)

Unicorn milk is unbelievable stuff; the highest of the twenty-nine *angelical liquors* in the flawed enumeration of Averroes. The resolutely bovine get a spiteful buzz in the small of their backs by saying it's no better than cow's milk, and that a unicorn far from being more than a cow, is but a cow, one horn the less. Still, purists compare it with a woman's milk and to the upbeat it gives joy. And, but like most incredible things, it's hard to come by. This is how you must get it. First, go into the woods, the darker the better, though not too dark to see. Clawing wet cobwebs from your face, find a place where curdled fog-streamers are lapped in the inguinal folds of branches, and it smells of mud, fern, Spanish chestnut and honeysuckle. The thrushes and the blackbirds sing, but quietly and sadly, and slowly, and at a deeper pitch, so that it sounds not like singing at all, but moaning.

The unicorns at first will look like mist, but glowing brighter than mist. Sometimes their horn is gilded and their mane is blond. This is a trick of the light tumbling as if down a chimney through the forest's needles, dusts, nests and leaves. What you have to do is to look fazed, in trouble, malfunctioning, forlorn. Tangled strands of thick hair blown across your face; some drops of blood tugged from your cheek by a bramble thorn; burrs, sedge and torn nettle-leaves caught both on your crushed-velvet skirt, which is a becoming bottle-green embroidered with wildflowers, and on your flame-coloured jerkin crudely sewn from enormous dead leaves. Something back to front or inside-out to your eyes. And even a fizz and soft sparks from the mussed or felted wiring, fine as hair and wrung by life from a rent in your neck. People who don't know what they are talking about say it is better to be a virgin. They are like those mushroom fanciers who spread self-interested disinformation. Because, no offence intended, soon a unicorn will come, perhaps several.

So—express delight, but in no more than a whimper, because however confidently they cluster round you, they are shy creatures and will soon bolt, even at the thudding of your own heart. Most unicorns have green, grey or brown eyes with vertical pupils and an alert, kindly gleam, not like a target or a cat. But what you want if possible is one with one green and one grey, one grey and one brown, or one brown and one green eye, shaded by thick white lashes. The black ones with dark green eyes are also special. So choose your unicorn, choose the very most best, and take it with you ever deeper into the forest, leading it by the kiss curl that curls down its forehead like a rill, until you find a glade where the sun glares through a sink-hole in the bluish canopy and warms and illuminates plump grass. Which, exactly like your skirt, is studded and spangled with cornflowers, bull-rushes and Indian corn, and pansies with smudged eyes, and dawn-coloured crocuses and unripe strawberries; and which looks as if lit from beneath, shining its own lime-green light (with purple patches) on the underside of the unicorn's belly and the frog of your chin. But which gives with a shuddering squelch making brown water trickle around your unicorn's feverish hooves, clumsy and much too big, not canted but drummed, shaded with white fetlock, and the colour of scorched amber. A hollow boom betrays, beneath the saturated grass, the existence of dry rooms filled with twigs and leaves.

Now, curry comb, hoof pick, dandy brush. Fetlock, withers, pastern, rump. There is a Dobbin or even Boxer quality to unicorns, and they will stand still, their legs planted wide and their ears swivelling pleasantly, to be groomed or, later, when you have their trust, ridden. The next bit is the tricky bit. Can you bear to kiss their hot, pink lips, not glazed like our lips, but made of marshmallow skin with stray white hairs, and flobbery. Though mild, they are simple beasts, and sometimes they will think you are giving them sugar and try to nibble off your nose not out of malice but stupidity. Kiss their lips, caress their ears, suck on curly strands of mane, and even tail, out of which if you like you can fashion a living wig and a false moustache, and make them close their eyes by kissing their felted eyelids and blowing along their lashes, whilst all the time (behind your back) hiding a suede bridle inlaid with zinc-plated suns and copper gibbous moons, and fitted with a silver-gilt *art-nouveau* Pelham bit adorned with figurines of wood and water nymphs or, if you cannot afford one of those, a bridle made from binder-twine, its reins not plaited but strung, more loosely than a violin bow, with not blond but blonde hair, or black or auburn or grey. The bit must not jingle, nor must your nerves. So, go on caressing the unicorn's ears, but quietly slip the bridle up its face, over the rifled, twisted, barley-sugar-scented horn, clear as a feverish icicle of Coca-Cola, only not frosted, not unlike a lolly un-sucked.

Rub its kiss-closed eyes and caressed yet swivelling ears.

Then use your gentle thumb and forefinger in the corners of its lips to open the mouth for the bit. It will shake its head, breathe grassy breath in your face, and pull back, and rear perhaps, but this is a formality. Last but not least, the milk. If you go on caressing your unicorn's ears, it will grow languid and lie itself down in the grass, tuck its hooves with their polished copper shoes under its neat belly, and dreaming it stumbles, will twitch and brace itself in a hypnic jerk. Its breathing slows and you can slip the bridle off (you won't need that anymore) and the unicorn, bridle-less and suddenly resembling a naked woman without her glasses, will toss its head, though without conviction. Then you can blow the conch you have hidden in your clothes, part your own legs, lifting crushed-velvet skirts in ruched swags like a safety curtain to your two hips, one on each side, as milky as unicorn pelt themselves and forming with your milky legs a kind of proscenium arch with a high escutcheon or cartouche. Then, after coating it in your living spit, just as you slick an udder with its own milk, impale yourself so, so slowly, in starts and fits. The sensation for the unicorn is the sweetest in the universe, and it will be yours to take home and keep. But be careful. The point is sharp. Unicorn horn can be really, really sharp.

And also brittle. It can easily snap. Or also melt.

Or buckle and crimp.

Or even split. Think about it.

¡Marla!

Between the roses and the breaking waves.
(Calasso, *The marriage of Cadmus and Harmony.*)

Woken by someone touching me. His beard, printing suggestive squiggles in the inflamed skin of my face.

Caught in the beard, like scraps of food, was a gunmetal sky. With the smelly sun flaring through in scribbly filaments of copper, garnet and steel.

His green eyes kind now, even humane, yet upside down—beard was hair, and hair beard. Priapic nose, flanged, and within the beard or hair a wet-lipped mouth, engorged, flapping above my forehead in syncopated ululation.

As I lifted my nauseous body onto two elbows, my eyes rolling like fruit in a machine, he gambolled away, splashing through wavelets, his buttocks fleeced in black whorls, both in the dimples and also on the crests where, were they breasts, the nipples might be.

At a safe distance he turned, hesitant, wry, and chanted again, knuckles cocked on his hips, and I saw his un-inflated penis peeping from pubic thatch, resting horizontal on plump retracted balls and mirroring, in the polished plane of his nippled chest, his nose and eyes. He intoned once more and was off, high-stepping through the sunlit fire of the waves, or wading powerfully, his arms and hips swinging like someone's with a hula-hoop. Or otherwise out of the water and skipping sideways, throwing up his arms with each skip, along the strand, until he became insectile with distance and disappeared at a spit where pines kissed the sea.

I had been dreaming I was sweating, on pine-needles, in a matted forest—the crooked, rosy-barked trees festooned with mistletoe and lichen—and all night my blanket kept sliding off. Before me, in a clearing, lay the manhole cover, opened onto a bottle-shaped pit, around the cast-iron rim of which a wonderfully scuzzy lamb, its legs as long and dangling as a soft toy's, was dancing and gambolling, tossing its head about.

But now I saw I was lying not on pine-needles but sand, and warmish seawater was scurrying up and back over my legs. This was the sliding blanket of the dream. As for the lamb on the rim of the pit, who knows whether that was the gambolling stranger, or perhaps even me. I'd shat myself too, it seemed—my sodden, baby-blue trousers were stained and bulked with spreading halos in olive and orange.

A few yards out, awash, was the maroon roof of a car with an overweening gull planted at its edge. It was minutely fluted, this edge, like the crust of a pie or a bottle-top. The car made gurgles and plops as the waves passed through the open windows. Some poor sod had parked in the water. And clenching my stomach so as not to barf, I rose slowly and lifting bent knees, a pantomime creeper, splashed towards it into the sea.

The car was empty of course. *Of course* because as always, if you don't know who the patsy is, it's you. I was the poor sod. The car, rocking gently like a sunken boat, was mine.

Its insides, with neatly folded drifts of sand, and lighted ball-bearings bubbling from its seats, glowed with a blue faint light, studded with pulsing transparent shrimpy things. A floating cassette-tape, partly unravelled, black with a handwritten silver legend, tapped at the windscreen. The wing mirrors displayed the mirrored underside of the surface of the sea, and had attracted swarms of pale squashy worms which threatened—this made my stomach spasm—unexpectedly to assemble themselves into letters and words.

Over the mirrors meant
To glass the opulent
The sea-worm crawls—grotesque, slimed, dumb, indifferent...

Clinging to the armrest of the door through its open window, for its reassuring texture alone, I opened my mouth as if to sing, spraying not music but chunky sick across the glistening roof. The observant gull swapped off-hand calm for an instant tensioned quiver and wolfed the larger lumps down, pausing, when further gulls bombed, to shriek, crouch, and brace its spumy wings. And from the night before, in flashback, cued by wing, I suddenly remembered this—ribbed and melodramatic clouds, barring a pulsing moon.

Lowering my trousers in the water, and stepping out, I allowed them, undulating beneath the chiselled surface, to waft away. Their languor was that of a manta. In the pockets had been only a sodden paper coaster from *Marlita's Bar,* with a pale blue trident motif, depicted on a fluttering flag. On it was written in a loopy script, its dots circles, its periods hearts, soaking into the fibrous paper, girlish and mad—

¿Borrachito? Wake up, wake up!
¡Bestial! Cu l8r al Calvarí.
Celaje, ocaso. ¡Mental! COME! Be there!!!
Besos (¿¿¿y lo demás???), ¡Marla!

And on the back —

¡Oye! Your cat is in the sea. Get over it.
¡Que Cenegal! Bestezuela. Whatever.
Calvarí, SUNSEt, *touching the Bark of the cypress tree.*

Pps. ¿Bestial, No?

She, if it was a she who had written this, which by the writing it couldn't not be, clearly meant *car.* I don't have a cat, didn't at least. Creepy, even curious, that the scored blue marks on a paper coaster could convey this urgent, unknown voice, but in a language I did not wholly understand. And— *touching the bark of the cypress tree ... ?*

The keys were in the ignition, but I could have guessed it wouldn't start. Wouldn't even turn over. So—coming out of the sea in the sun, exhausted, vented, and a watery sparkler attached to each of the sand-coloured hairs on my belly, arm, leg. A stinking reed, hollow from end to end, and flushed through with soil, like our progenitors those mirror-dwelling worms, I now wanted only to gambol in wavelets and run the tide-line of the beach, with its offerings of broken flip-flops, ping-pong balls (?!) and sun-crisped weed.

Because—bugged in retrospect by the naked man who had woken me, and especially his ululations. Beardless as I was, on either chin or buttock, nevertheless I found myself thudding the beach with my feet as I too ran, leaning into the centre of a spiral which had nonetheless been straightened out, like a party-horn.

Now—a flooded car, no trousers, but a lettuce-coloured cardigan, not mine, half-buried in sand. Which would not come out when pulled. And had to be dug out with the acetate sole of a high-heeled shoe. Also a neatly folded tweed jacket with mannered malachite buttons. Also I had a date for later, as I understood it, *touching the bark of the cypress tree,* with someone called *¡Marla!* Shaking out sand and holding it upside down, I buttoned the cardigan up to its neck and fed my legs into the arm holes, an old trick, and over it wore the tweed jacket with its malachite buttonry. Too small for me, so my arms went out horizontally like a flying child.

The thing about black-outs is that, if you can't remember having them, you *can* tell that continuity has got it wrong. Without the blackout, continuity also gets it wrong, but never with this abandon and scope. And perhaps continuity is being merciful—if it is true that what is not boring is agony.

There is a theory that you murder to justify your pre-existing guilt. Unsure where this might lead, I certainly felt, besides the nausea, lessened now by having thrown-up, a slicing remorse, as if I had willed-up something really bad on some innocent out of pure spite. Another thing—*her* colours were hyper-bright.

Because behind me a rubble boathouse, sinking cockeyed into sand, was plastered with ranks of identical posters, pinked and frilled by the wind, so that I imagined I had woken with compound eyes, or wearing a kaleidoscope. They were glued to the blistered green door and sandy wall, and even, beside it, up the creased rosy trunks of neighbouring pines.

Repeated again and again in guileless silk-screened colours, the poster-girl had a white face and green hair. The stalk of her red beverage-parasol pierced a red blob and a green. A red treble-clef of a drinking-straw; red inflected lips beneath a nose defined only by red nostrils; shades, indicated by brown lenses and worn low on the nose so that navy eyes glowed over them. A navy swim-dress set off childish arms and paper-white skin, teeth, corneas. In the same chemical red as her lips, grained, so as to have been kissed-out in lipstick letters, was the hand-cut loopy legend—

¡Marlitas Es Lo Que Te Gusta Mas!
¡Marlitas' is what you like so much!
¡Marlitas es Was wünschen Sie!

My body knew something I didn't know, my eyes knew more than me. Which was that this unknown ¡Marla!, with whom I appeared to have a date, touching the bark of the cypress tree—*was* the poster-girl.

And was also—it was coming back to me—the person I'd seen only the night before. With her pukka tweed jacket, itchy submariner's polo-neck stained with a few drops of coffee, torn jeans through which scuffed knees glowed as—her hair aloft and waving in curled hanks—she walked along the seafront on smoking sand.

Ragged, washed-out waves were snatching at her green bovver-boots, and above her, signs, masts, street-lamps were rocking and pinging in the unusual wind. There was some kind of registration problem—the sand had banked up on the road, gobs of surf fell across it with the clicking sound of knitting, but it looked as if she wasn't touching down, and it also looked as if the signs were swinging and clanking not in the wind but because of her.

The boy whose hand she held was trying only to hold her down, to stop her blowing away. This could just have been the way she walked, her blue-jean back-pockets swelling, beneath the sturdy hem of tweed, and reinforced with a thrifty piping of dried leather.

The pouncing sea, white with hollow bubbles, but also marbled with a jellied blue-green, had borrowed its colours from her eyes.

Later on that night—last night, it must be now, subject to how long I'd been out of it—in some bar I'd found her—who knows where or how. Seated on a red stool in the form of a scalloped bottle-top, her jaw propped moodily by one hand, she had, in a self-conscious aping of the poster, picked up her glass, hollowed out her cheeks, and dipped her face but not her eyes (stark, famished) to nibble for a drinking-straw shaped as a treble-clef.

And with those eyes still peeping sideways under her sand-coloured eyebrows, motionless even when her face trembled, with an affectation of poise, she had turned the mussed yellow hair of the back of her head to me so as to watch me sway amongst the letters of the word *Bocadillos,* formed in *Windowlene* in her own loopy script with its circles and hearts, on the mirror behind the shelves of coloured bottles.

I took a neighbouring bottle-top. She ducked a flap and rose up slowly behind the bar.

—*¿Dos Equis?*

And she had placed before me the same puffed, frilled bar-mat I was later to find in my pocket, embossed with a royal-blue barbed trident in its centre, displayed on a fluttering flag.

—*Sí, gracias.*

Would the next question, I wondered, be whether I could also say *No?* Because this was the kind of girl, I feared, to look at that racy, assenting face, who was, as they used to say in those less guilty times, all throttle and no brakes.

The beer sighed as she levered off the cap, which she flicked in the air and caught behind her back, and it sighed again in the glass she then poured. The bottle too was flipped behind her back and landed precisely in a PVC dustbin where it broke against the hulls of other bottles.

Squatting on bouncy, widened knees down behind the bar—if I leaned over I could just see her—she tinkered with the sound system, and on came some mournful yowling type.

You know baby,
Don't you know,
Bay-a-be?
I could neverLet you go
Down without
A song!
Oh no-ho,
No-ho,
No!

—*¿Inglés?* she asked, suddenly popping up.
—*Sí.*
—*¡El Reino Unido!* she exclaimed.
—*Sí.*
—*Gran Bretaña.* She saluted and stood up straight.
—*Sí.*

And now she raised her finger, comically, drew in her cheeks again and added with manic shifting eyes and a fixed grin—

—*¿Dios Salve La Regina, no?*

—*Sí.*
—*No hay futuro. Es una régimen fascista,* she sang, fairly tunelessly. Me too,

she added in a Lancastrian voice. I'm British too. Like you I mean. If Lancashire's allowed, pet?

That made me laugh, despite the fear I felt at her looks, her visible speed, her mysterious candour. As for the fear, I felt like a kitten dabbing at a joggled woollen ball, jade green like her cardigan, and dabbing it with outstretched claws, and missing, and it should have been fun, but I was scared.

—At least, me mum is. Or imagines she is, she's not no more, or she is, but *it* isn't. You're a long way from Lancashire now, ducks. And you're no bottle-blonde picture-postcard treat who works *op t'mill* no more neither, whatever you say you are. But me, now me, no *I* don't *believe* in nations. I'm not even an object, let alone a subject. *I* rule the waves, mine at least. Who on earth would want to rule someone else's? Someone called nationalism the V. D. of humanity. Or something like...? Or was that war? Or measles? By other means? Can't remember anyway. What's your name, pet? But ...
—?
—Sorry, I had to let it out. Nobody except Jesús has been in all day. Jesús, the *shite!* How could he! *Why'd you do what you did?* I still can't believe it how could the little shite. *Ay que es sucio y tan feo.* Yuk! Repulsive.
—Weird name!
—Jesús? Every pretty, vacant boy in this hell-hole's called Jesús—unless it's María. Or Chucho.

Then she took a fold of my cheek and waggled it in her fingers.

—And so I've been dying for someone to talk to! And here you are, just like that, pet! It's like magic.

And as for me—vertigo, which is to say an essential un-safety, which wobbled my red bottle-top, yet was seated not in me but the universe, as if I myself was looking down at this trembling town, between the purring, pulsing sea and the conical hill—complete with nippled convent—*its* enigmatic, continual clanging of bells, like a works—plus a coarse spiral scar of road on a second hill, well behind it, where the new *urbanización* was a-building. And between sea and convent, the minute picture-window of this bar, lit with a yellow torch-bulb, with its toy-like figures, flimsy, stiff as pipe-cleaners, one perching artfully on a bottle-top, the other tinkering again with the music machine.

When music duly resumed, she put her elbows on the dulled zinc, and making clam-shell hands supported her fragile jaw.

—This job stinks, she said. I mean it totally sucks.
—I'll drink to that.
—Amuse me, come on!

—Amuse me! I'm bored shitless.

—You're wasting my time, she sang or taunted, but she was smiling. I always think of the shape of an hourglass when I say that, she said. The waist of time, I mean. And there's no time to waist. We are fleeting creatures. The waist of time is just the present moment. What do you have to say to me *now?* Before the end of the universe, i.e. our lives. Come on, out with it, what you got to tell me?

—Cat got your tongue?

Clearly she went fast, and not down any road.

—Cat's got his tongue! Cat's got his tongue!

And she was chanting this with a provocative, almost an aggressive, but also a desperate smile and lilt. And, her eyes rounded, and glossy not sparkling, and beginning to be a little bloodshot, she made a frog *moue,* her chin resting on her palms again, and lengthening her eyes with her fingers, stared at me.

She yawned ecstatically, one hand out to the side rapidly fanning her mouth.

—Let's seal it with a *Freixenet,* she said suddenly, her eyes still watering from the yawn. Don't fret, 'tis on the house, she added in an impossibly low voice. But I *must* have it. I demand *Freixenet!*
—Seal what?
—Friendship? Don't knock it. Anyhow—Jesús, is a little *shite.*

Small fierce grass-fires flared up and died down in her eyes. And she took up a misted or shot-blasted bottle and making a double chin while thrusting up the centre of her mouth, popped off the cork with her fingers, neatly felling, it was a direct hit, the polycarbonate treble-clef straw-dispenser from its glass shelf. She didn't pick them up.

But poured two wide shallow glasses, so the sticky, fizzy stuff slopped over their edges and bubbled on the dulled, glass-marked zinc, but also splashed across her jeans with the torn out knees. She clicked me a outsized wink and chinked glasses, wetting both our fingers, and tossed hers off before pouring more.

—Fab! she said.
—I have to drive?
—Oh no you don't! she warned in sing-song. Anyways, it's on the house. Take it or leave it! And taking it is what Marla recommends.

Now, hunching her back she tried not to burp, or perhaps she was trying to.

—It's your funeral, I'm telling you. I mean!, she said.

—Seriously, she added, I've been knocking it back all day. With Jesús and without! Same difference, actually!

Trying to burp.

—What else am I supposed to do?, she complained.
—I'd never have guessed. My tone was cheap and crabbed. *Why am I so cheap* I thought, but didn't say.
—No, she said, seriously, goes with holding down the job, holding down the al-co-hol. And holding off the punters, too, she said, wagging her heavy, delightful finger at me.

And she burped gloriously, succeeding at last. Tried and failed to burp again. And sang a few bars of *Ghost Town.*

—Because, she told me earnestly, it's true, this *is* nothing but a *ghost town—ooo, woo!*

Now she was piercing an olive with a cocktail parasol, but it kept slipping away. But once she'd pierced it, she pierced a glacé cherry from a jar, which kept bobbing around. And then nibbled and licked at them absently for a while, her eyes unfocused, and when she'd eaten them away, she used the parasol to pick her teeth. She'd gone someplace else, though she was staring at me.

And then she shivered all down her body, trying to return to it.

And turning her back, on the far side of the bar, she rested her hands behind her, levered her behind onto the zinc, and pressing her ankles together, swung her legs over it, landing neatly on flexing if scuffed and bony knees on my side. And as if it were a red mushroom, flecked in white, she clambered back onto her bottle-top.

—Now that's what I call crossing the bar, she said, perching there and rubbing her hands up and down the blue-jeaned shins she'd clasped to her breasts.
—*And may there be no moaning of the bar, when I put out to sea,* I quoted. Is that what you mean?
—*Over the bar* in that poem means dying. Over the bar in a book means it's readable—some hope! Over the bar—in here—meaning I don't bother to go under it!' She made her voice deep to say under. 'But stand on my tippy toes to rest the lip of *ma derrière* upon it, then holding my ankles together just so, I simply *flip!* them over it *comme ça!* Landing—*voila!*—elegantly enough beside my best and only punter, *qui est peut-être un peu, parce que todo es, verdaderamente* under the bar, *cariño mío!* God you're cute, she said.

The *Freixenet* she'd spilled from the glasses was smoking on the counter. She laughed in preparation, then poured two mounds of sugar in the middle of the *Freixenet,* and made spirals up them in runny honey borrowed from her cocktail-making stash.

—*Monte Caracol,* she said, *Monte Calvarí,* and the sea. It was a relief-map of the town and the hills, one behind the other, which wedged it down against the coast. The larger, more distant of the two, Caracol, unlike Calvarí had no convent, but you sensed its loss, it's absence—the brilliant air was charged with the missing shape. They also, like breasts in this, were uneven, and one set further back. All the summer visitors noticed it, and seemed unable to resist remarking on it, especially, interestingly enough, the women. While the coarse wags, drinking their brandy with their coffee of a morning in the smoke-wreathed *Club Nacional,* likened the hills not to breasts, but buttocks, distorted in the manner of that unmentionable traitor, Picasso, but—and with a whorled hair of mattas—a maquis-like scrub which was very un-Picassoesque. The hills were in reality, as the cutaway and carefully labelled postcard sold in the souvenir shops explained, volcanic plugs or something, and the immense bay, a crater lake. Only, this minor bar-top sea was yellow—and in this light, so too were her revolving eyes.

—*And here are you and here are me,* she went on, creating *us* between coast and hill with dabs of honey, displaying, meanwhile, an exile's fascination with cheap rhymes and puns. And this is where, her hair trembling in the plane of her face, she leaned her face towards mine—so I could feel its heat—closed her eyes, which made me accidentally purse my lips and—laughing madly drew suddenly back.

—Hel-lo? Come in Houston! What planet am I on please advise? she asked.

—I mean!, she said. Hel-lo?

—You *thought* you was going to *kiss* me!, she said. Guy walks into a bar, hits on barmaid, who hinted delicately at friendship, and imagines he's going to *kiss* me!

Her wide mouth wide-open, displaying plenty of small plump teeth, between reddening lips. Her palms open too like a platter on which she slid her head from side to side.

Dangerous—something of a naked flame here, in an incendiary mood.

Then she picked up the *Freixenet* bottle and, saying *Blah blah blah-bitty blah,* poured some in her lap, where it fizzed briefly and disappeared, and she started giggling manically, throwing her eyes about and moving her head, and the wings of her shoulders now, as if she was dancing.

—*Mira,* she said, seriously we'll have *Bombardini.* We all drink it. So numbingly *good!* And she ducked behind the bar again, waddling slightly—her trousers were wet—was she completely mad—or was it that sensation of *whatever* kind was the whole point? With a rapping of filters she prepared *espressos,* and started shaking up her mix.

—It's something like a *zabaglione* made with *Avocaat,* espresso and sugar. *¡Toma!*

And when I hesitated

—*¡Mira!* she said, slurring plaintively a little, this is on the *house.* Everything, but *everything* is on da house. Play your cards right, she said, with a long gritted smile.

Then, seating herself again beside me, with a squelch, on top of her outsize bottle-top barstool, she upended her *bombardino* too, into her lap, and this time by accident it seemed.

—Shite! she said. Fuck!

For a second she was livid and again—I was still more scared.

—¿Tienes coche? she was asking. Tengo que quitarme mis blue-jeans. They're a sight. ¡Pero no mirarás,! she said, ¡Y no tocarás mis mamelles!

And with a finger she closed each of our four eyes, first hers and, feeling the way slowly, then mine. I didn't know what *all* her words meant, but they sure sounded, and even tasted, good in her mouth—better even than *Freixenet.* Because this time we did kiss, electric and chaste. And unreal. When she opened her eyes again she smiled in fondness and then made a funny face like someone playing with a baby. But her voice was deeper than it might have been in an ideal world and I suddenly found myself thinking—she can't be a boy?

—Let's go, she said.

The dark *Bombardino* she'd spilt on herself was chromatographing her crotch.

—Don't we tidy up first? I asked.

She didn't answer, but moving sideways along it pumping her snow-plough hands back and forth, she swept bottles, glasses and ashtrays over the back edge of the zinc where you could hear but not see them bounce, jingle, crash. At the end of her run she collided with one of the bottle-top bar stools, and it swung majestically from side to side before going over and rolling back and forth.

—Guess what, she said, I'm smashing. Don't you think I'm smashing? Would you agree. *¡Venga!,* you have to agree, no? I'm smashing. Call me smashing, 'cos that's my name.

And so, with a clacking of padlocks and lengths of metal, efficient yet strangely humiliating, this sudden submission to form at last, she dropped and secured the steel roller-shutters and shut-up shop.

Only, my car wouldn't start. So leaving the picnic she'd gathered up for us plus her suede crescent-moon shoulder-bag on the back seat, we ran along pushing it. Until, hopping on one foot, I yanked myself in and thrust it into second whilst she clung onto the bumper and, giggling, crying and choking, was dragged slowly on her belly through the sand-drifts that coated the road, still smoking in a trail behind us, not where the wheels had rolled, but only between them, where she'd lain.

When I halted, gunning the engine, she climbed in, tears in wandering tracks down sand-dusted cheeks, muted at last by a profound, thrilled joy. We drove slowly through dimness, street-lamps sliding solemnly back to either side of us, eventually to be replaced by trees, and our wipers smearing the windscreen with dry dust and the gunge of flies.

—Hey! *¡Párate!* Halt! she was saying, flapping her spread fingers, her lips tubed, and bouncing on the car seat as if there was something too hot in her mouth. We were here! Because through the smeary windscreen was the very same cockeyed boat-house where I had woken just now, half-lying in the sea! Pasted with its poster-girl posters, surrounded by fly-posted pines, the sea itself beyond it lapping at banks of shingle and sand with the sound of a cat, milk. Only now, then, i.e. last night, it had been dark. The sand-strewn road petered amongst bright garbage and mounds of mud. Revving the engine to mount the curb, I pulled onto the sidewalk, crushing the wild asparagus sprouting through the gravel.

By the light of the headlamps, dust flowed over the sand, though the wind had dropped. Excited by the light, shrimp-like bugs began zinging, coupling, feasting, expiring in their thousands all around us as we drove. Sagging branches were drawn like fingernails along the painted roof of the car.

Though the promoters of this particular *urbanización* had already lost heart, like those of a ship, sunk long since but seen through translucent wavelets, its lamps still faintly burned. Desolation, and truer a solitude than ever is found in un-raped nature. The motionless pines which crowded us and ran in both directions along the shore were rank with mosquitoes singing in minute but frissile chords. Either *Marla y Jesús*, or *M & J*, or an arrow-transfixed heart, was sprayed in silver on the bark of many of the pine trees there, and even on the vine-clad rear wall of the listing boathouse—half-buried as it was, like Ozymandias himself, in sand. And even, with some violence, malice—across *her* face on sample posters.

Above us, brighter than all the others though these too were bright, brighter even than the uncertain and varying street-lamps—was the evening star.

—Look, it's Jesús again. He's *pining* for me, *boom-boom!*, she said, pointing to one of his tagged pines. What a *shite!* I still can't *believe* he could do that to me. You're no Jesús, friend, but something tells me, something *yells* me, you'll do!

Her hair both curled, frisée almost, and quivering, so that the waves in her hair were also dancing a second order dance. Standing up straight from her high forehead like a lion's, it was only with difficulty flattened down at the sides. The greenish colour of lions—of dried grass and sand. Her face, the face of a starlet—beauty distorted by its own winning speed. Sometimes a lock would fall across her face and compressing her lips she'd blow it back with her mouth. Sometimes locks rose up in the still air on their own, like caterpillars.

As feast she'd brought another bottle of *Avocaat* and a bottle of *Malibu*, and a third unidentified bottle, bulbous in the manner of a Mandelbrot set, and olives, almonds, bread, tomatoes, garlic, oil, salt, a cold omelette, and tiny plastic cups. A *Thermos* of coffee. And a *Tupperware* box of ice. Plus red, treble-clef straws—three of them?—and a bunch of cocktail parasols. And tooth-picks for the olives. And a wedge of frilly white paper coasters with *Marlita's* on them in powder-blue. Playing at picnics, she spread her tweed jacket, with its oversized malachite buttons, and neatly laid out the meal, whispering to herself as she placed each thing. The crickets were chattering like teeth in the darkness, in time to, above our heads, the rippling stars. The air smelt of myrrh and rotting seaweed and though the sea was dark, the street-lamps, wavering brighter and dimmer, as if the hand on the rheostat were a lush's, piped and gilded the chipped edges of each surging wave. Later, the moon rose behind repetitive barred clouds in the form of a rib-cage, and far out and long ago, a liner must have passed, because the routine breathing of the sea got faster, and went unsteady, like panting more.

—All my girlfriends are asking—but is he the one? she told me. Yes he is the one, she said with asperity, but not the *only* one. Why, why, why does there have to be just *one*. Do they all come from families of only children? she asked. I mean!
—It's just like the one and the many—I said—the one gets you into all

sorts of tangles, and so do the many, but maybe less.
—You're so sharp you'll cut yourself, she said.

And she pulled a reefer out of the bottomless, gibbous-moon bag, some matches you could strike on a zip, and a handful of loose pills she was keen we should share. I wondered if they weren't vitamin pills. She clearly lived as if time, like a pot of red paint, were running out. And was right to trust that the faster she painted, the more paint would be left.

She was still wearing jeans sodden and stained in the lap where, madly, if excess exuberance could ever be mad, she had poured her *Freixenet* and spilt her *Bombardino.* It's as if all these innocent liquors could not but be drawn there, to suckle themselves. Now she turned the jeans up at her ankles, took off the green cardy, with its horn buttons and nothing underneath—however deep voice she wasn't after all a boy—and, laying it down in the sand, bare-footed, she padded into the waves. She turned to face me, crossed her arms on her naked breasts like a corpse, and fell stiffly backwards into the water. She came up, bobbing on the surface like a plank, her eyes shut and her mouth open, then crouched to rise to her feet with water streaming from her pockets, her mouth, and her hair. Which had formed into flat curls like a blonde spaniel's.

—As you have probably have not guessed yet, Dawn, that's mum if you must know, I call her Dawn 'cos that's her name, like, first come here as an exotic dancer at *Puppy Love,* she explained, streaming back up the banks of shingle and mounds of sand towards me for another swig of *Malibu,* which she gargled with appreciatively. Appraising for a moment the representation of her own dim face on the ranked posters, she squatted abruptly beside me, one cheek resting on one knee and her eyes dreaming. Her drying curls hung down to one side, so the fragile back of her neck and the ankle-bone lump at the base of her skull showed.

—So when Dawn gets all snobby about Jesús I say—well cool it Dawn you're only an exotic dancer blown-in from Lancashire. *And* a bottle-blonde. At least Jesús wants his own handyman company. Dawn was reacting, you see, against the claustrophobia of her orthodox childhood. Her Papá was a vicar as I picture it—she won't say. And that's how I got the modelling job, is through Dawn. For the posters, I mean, and she gave a languid, backhanded wave to the tattered psychedelic face repeated manyfold. They used a computer and did it from a photo. They built their brand around me. *Marlita's!* It's not that I look like the posters—but the other way round, they look like me. Then when we'd done the posters, well, they thought, they might as well, they went and got me to run the venue!

—Papá's an architect, she added. From Bremen. Once upon a time. Papá don't believe in walls. We believe our walls 'n ceilings exist, he says. But now if we didn't, our homes would be unlivable. We also forget what is inside the walls—the meat of the house means nothing to us, only its surfaces. Names of things in general are more often the names of shapes than meats. I find it über-painful to visualise what is inside my walls, or even my wife. They parted company way back of course and went their own separate ways. Except for me you'd never know they'd ever been an item. He's doing the *urbanización* on the *Caracol* with Claus and Miguel, his golfing-buddies. That's his day job. It's make or break, probably make. Then he can build shitloads of houses without walls, and one for me, she said, her cheek still rested sideways on the knees she was clasping with her arms. Her face with a simper which had uncertainty and fear congealed within it, perhaps because she was so young. Drawing a languid spiral on my chest she added—
—To have babies in.

—Before being an architect, she went on, he was a balloonist in some orchestra.
—Bassoonist?
—That's what I said! *Der Orkester der Stadt*, was what it was called, he told me. His mamá and papá were expats, they came from Munich post-war, she said. Papá only followed later on, when he decided to retrain, and that's how he met Dawn, one fateful night at *Puppy Love!* Hence me!

—Poor Papá. How he loves me. When I was little I asked him, if the sky is so beautiful, why can't I go there. You will, one day, he told me, and I couldn't see why he was so earnest, fretful, sad. He kept pointing upwards, but unable to speak. His nose started running. And his glasses misted. He was like that all day, just sobbing occasionally. He calls me *Madame Marla Maid*, sort of like marmalade. By the way I *adore* marmalade, if you're thinking of prezzies.
—Or parlour maid
—Cruel!
—!
—Be cruel again please. *Please!*

—?
—Brrr. Overdue costume change, she said.

She drew down her jeans with difficulty—they'd shrunk on her legs as if painted on, and could only be peeled inside out. She was hopping about in the sand.

Also something luminiferous about her knickers, despite their *Bombardino* stains, as if they were emitting or transmitting light, which is impossible, so it must have been an ingredient in the washing powder reacting with the dim, pulsing street-lamps and the stars.

They were thick, glowing, opaque, trunk-like, and pulled high on her belly, like a lady's. These she took off too and threw them amongst the trees. In her crescent-moon shaped leather shoulder-bag had been a flimsy silk dress cut in such a way that when she dropped it into place over her upstretched arms, shaking her head as it came out, her breasts beneath it seemed only glued to her chest, and her hips brittle.

Her bare legs emerged from its hem. Her shins and calves she kept mainly in the water now as we spoke, and drank, clawing at shingle with spread toes. The long wait for each wavelet to pounce on the tawny sand, before soaking away into it. Each time the surface of the water fell back, a garter-shaped band at a different level on each of her cocked legs was varnished by the morose street-lamps, and the rising moon. She clearly liked to feel the feebly-lapping surf on the backs of her knees and, lifting the flimsy dress higher up, slopping between her legs with the *pocking*, gurgling slaps you hear beneath a pier or a boat.

The patches of shingle, plus the patches of sand which, like bald patches under a comb-over, continued beneath the pines, the banks of mottled purple and white shells, the mounds of plastic bottles—so, the meticulous sea!

While her wispy silk dress, a bluish-maroon with small sprigs of roses and bluebells printed on it, but spread randomly, the randomness repeating like old wallpaper, was rolled up above her navel now and her fresh greenish skin glowed in the dawn.

A tramp or liner, its lights still burning, was drawn slowly along the horizon.

And she rolled her silk dress up to her neck and waded further in, and there was something about the sea that seemed to clasp her round her hard, hollow waist. So that I feared, and the fear was real fear, that she was already spoken for, and by a diviner nobody than me.

—Don't get that wet too. It's all you've got.

I meant the silk tunic or dress, but like the little boy who didn't care, she said—

—I. don't. Care.

For the first time, in the short time I'd known her, she was serious, her wide smile closed down into a mild frown. So taking off my clothes I slid down the shingle to join her. We moved slowly in water which—like life!—had lukewarm compartments, and sudden compartments of ice, and I could feel the tide pulling us outwards.

—So I call this, she said, dribbling salt-water, swimming out to *see*. Let's never come home, lets swim out to *see*. You get? Swimming out to *see*. Come with me, go on, and *see*. Have you never wanted to swim and swim and swim and swim? she asked. And swim. And swim. Forever? Never turning back? You see! You see!

Salted, stiff wavelets spat only semi-pleasantly in my face.

—Because we've come to *see*, she said. To *see*, amongst other things, the ghosts that are everywhere around us, the undead, otherwise known as *people*. And this town, she added bitterly, if you ask me, it's just one more garden of earthly fucking delights.

A fishy silence, followed by the sudden barking of a dog further along the shore.

—*Fornication avec l'onde*, or something—that's what someone or other called swimming, I told her.

She laughed brilliantly, but said while spitting out seawater—

—And yeah...
—Yeah?
—*Prefiero fornicaciòn avec l'ongle*, she said. *If* you ask me, she added, in the faded yet well-preserved Lancashire voice, which like her ringlets and her cruel and hungry beauty, she had presumably inherited from Dawn.

And she was laughing to herself again, in her light-headed, tipsy, irresponsible way. The loving Lancashire voice faintly globalised by music and films, even in other languages.

—*Y pues,* and trying not to laugh so that her virginal, gravid cheeks swelled, *avec le ... le ... dongle!*

We swam back. The sea hadn't sobered us. Marla, stooping and wet, rattled up the shingle and padded across sand and put on my shirt. What was I supposed to wear? My blue linen trousers. And it was warm here, under the layered blankets of mosquitos and stars. But she wanted to tell me something.

—Most people are just meat. No, nothing, but, I mean, she said.

I took her to be saying that only some have clocked where we are. The implied corollary being to dodge as much as you can of the meat, and hole up with those who, like her, swim out to *see.*

—Like papá's walls, she added, on reflection.

And first sat, then lay down, and rolled in a drift which had banked up against the door of the listing boathouse. She became a crumbly sand-sculpture, a decaying sandcastle-self. The effect, on her face especially, was to soften further her melting, mocking, butter-like features, so it was as if I were looking back in time at a girl from the past who *had* lived, and was now a weathered memory, the faintest contours on an eroded monument.

—Was that such a good idea? she asked, her hands on her behind and bouncing sanded buttocks in stiff, eccentric loops.

—Gritty, she said. Rhymes with pretty and yet.
—And what?
—Has such a different sound. You see, what things sound like depends on their meaning, she said seriously. And stately, she returned to the sea in a sandstone beige, and submerged, coming out again in skin-green.

Crossing her arms she peeled off my wet shirt, put on her tweed jacket, found faintly-greenish knickers in the bottomless moon-shaped suede shoulder-bag, fixed another *Bombardino,* with coffee from her *Thermos,* and started lobbing empty bottles at the sea.

The street-lamps finally went out. There was an instant now when divine fingers adjusted the pegs on the universe until things sang—the ponderous, tarnished orange moon; the whining, fleshy smoke of mosquitoes; the dull mineral smoke of sand; the ripples pouncing like kittens on the shingle; the smells of pine and tears and seawater and rotting seaweed and even drains; the syncopated throb of pulsing crickets and certain pulsing hearts; the alcoholic fizz of some tart, fermenting fruit, in the circumstances, the best smell in the universe; the identically dark profile of both the trembling mountains and her delivering face, cut-out of a still revolving sheet of stars. A gleam in one of her eyes, softened and sharpened with her mood, neatly completed the missing part of a famous constellation.

I shut my eyes and still saw stars. Someone clattered their claws quickly up my spine. It was Marla, being a crab, her face alight with mischief, joy. The sense of someone in charades madly trying to tell you something, their lips sealed but bulging, their eyes alight, and failing. How ever hard she tried, you were too slow, and didn't *get*, as Henry James would put it.

Then, she drank pure *Malibu*, and I drank pure *Avocaat*. Then she drank pure *Avocaat*, and I sampled *Malibu*. Then with her teeth she crunched up some of the last slivers of melting ice. She had to dull her star with drink because it burned too fast and bright. I lay on my back in the sand, Marla sitting on my hips like a succubus and grating the *Malibu* bottle-neck onto my teeth as the liquid glugged across my cheeks and up my nose. I tipped her over and sat on *her* hips, holding her wrists above her head, her giggles succeeded by the same quivering silence as when an angel supposedly passes overhead, though, admittedly, this one was underneath.

A long, fishy speechlessness on both our parts, followed by the sound of yet another wavelet pouncing on sand.

—*Mmmm*, she said eventually. *Mmmmm*... and suddenly toppled me and wriggled out. Her mouth was open as if she was trying to laugh, but she was laughing too hard to actually laugh. Amongst her teeth, some curdled *Avocaat*, pooling in her cat's tongue. Her lips, when she laughed, had a quality of being the same thickness all the way round, like those fishes who graze on the algae growing along the fish-tank glass, and lined as they were with plump, tube-like teeth, were maybe what gave her face the quality of being formally irresistible. But her lips were far from being enough to explain anything. If genius, like witchcraft, is where you can't see how it's done, there was plenty of this to both her face and her.

She wanted the jangling music from the car's brittle *hi-fi*, and while she was at it she switched on the headlamps which shone on a mound of old prams, casting *moirée* shadows through the dark wood. An extra-thick fog of mosquitos assembled, together with a variety of fluttering, furry moths. But a family of enterprising lizards, blown up mega-size as they flicked across the warming lenses of the headlamps, carried fan-like moth-wings in their mouths.

Marla poured a plastic beaker of olive oil, sliced a lemon, peeled a clove of garlic, and dared me to drink one, suck the second and chew the last.

—Thanks, but you first, I said,
—Then what are we playing for, she asked.
—Your body?
—My body? Shit no. *Hell* no. It's *your* body we are playing for. And she smiled, her eyes and teeth glowing and expanded, and drank the oil like a shot.
—*¡Venga!*, she said, wiping the back of her hand across her lips and trying to burp. Tastes like shite. *¡Mental!* Ouch. *J'ai envie de vomir*, she said, her cheeks vernal and swollen just above the ends of her lips. *¡Toma!*

She handed me my olive oil, heavy in its filmy medical dosing cup. *Jonestown*, was my last thought, as grateful, I drank.

Now she was taking the pale green knickers off. She carefully rolled-down the rim in her fingertips like a spliff, and lifting each knee unnecessarily high to press each breast, stepped first out of one leg-hole, then the other. The world was whirling round by now, as admittedly it always does, and besides, I was whirling the other way.

—Shit! *Venga, bicho*, you can sleep when you're dead, she said shaking me quite roughly. You can sleep all you like when you're dead! And she slapped my cheeks and laughed.

She had the bulbous bottle now, almost empty, flared and ribbed at the bottom, rising in a thin neck to a globular mouth, and she held this to her lips and drank.

—*Too drunk to fuck!* she sang, *too drunk to fuck!*

Her melted, blunted face, sweating like butter.

—*Grenadine.* A liquor or syrup made with pomegranates, I think, she said, consulting the side of the bottle. Like in the myth of Orpheus or somebody, she said.

Her hair was already dry and had gone the colour of pine-meat. She smelt of pine, or else the wood did, and also rotting seaweed. Her eyes, by a dawn just beginning to seep in off the sea, could be mistaken for nature-collages made from mist, frog-spawn, pine-needles. But her breasts were bigger than pine cones and her arms were shorter than branches and her hair was more enduring than surf. Her greenish skin softer than bark. On her head, I was so far gone, I could actually see a kind of raked coronet, just like that on the apex of the pomegranate shown on the side of the *Grenadine* bottle, whose label had a pomegranate shaped cut-thru to the pomegranate-coloured liquid which sloshed inside.

—It was pomegranate all along, not apple at all, that was the forbidden fruit of the world-famous, never-to-be-forgotten Garden of Eden, she informed me, taking my finger in hers and drawing it beneath the lamb-like swell of the underside of her belly, which felt like the softest stuff imaginable, so that you were hardly able to tell you were touching it. Papá told us that. Then she placed my finger in her mouth.

If people (by her mythology) are what souls look like, then she had an arresting one. It was not that she was a runaway train, only that inside her was a runaway train, trying to pierce her envelope, so that she had to move this envelope just as fast so as not to be pierced by the train. By envelope I mean greenish skin of course. Wet again of course, now that she had discarded the tweed jacket and gone back in, with those hard thighs, strung like bows, and grained with goose bumps in the dim dawn light. And by the train? What was the train if it wasn't *her?*

Wiping the back of her hand across her lips she came back up the shingle and sand to lift up my head, as I thought to kiss me, but she was forcing the mouth of the *Grenadine* bottle between my lips.

—*Mmmm?* she said. *Mmmmm...?*
—You're hurting me!

And I shook my head, the sticky red syrup spooling from the corners of my lips. I would drink the poisonous *Bombardini,* but drew a line at raw *Grenadine.*

And that was it. Nothing more.

Did we fuck? *Heaven* knows. Did we kiss again? Or maybe *hell.* And doubtless Marla too.

Later, like vomit, we would clear it up.

And how the fuck, incidentally, did my car get into the sea?

I felt a need to know.

Because usually when something important happens, someone remembers it. This was like an unremembered dream, but much too significant to forget. Forgotten, it had never happened at all, and that wasn't on. Plus I wanted to put *unrequited* dream and it could well be, given the dire state, thanks to her, I was in, that it was that. I would ask her in a bit, if she showed, I thought—because the awed sea was falling silent as, not for the first time, dusk too fell. Here on the very same shore, but today now, it was already growing dimmer. The sun shone low through pines. The mosquitoes awoke and began to fume, the sand to smoke. Wavelets pouncing. Time to move, I realised. The invitation, scribbled in her loopy script on the paper coaster had been—Monte Calvarí, at sundown, *touching the bark of the cypress tree.*

The twin conical hills placed on the littoral plain, were lopsided as to altitude—the further, *Monte Caracol,* dwarfing the nearer *Calvarí*—and tinkered with your sense of magnitude, distance, horizontality—hinting at the haywire and the ridiculous. But then, dressed in an inverted green cardigan and Marla's tweed jacket, my arms outstretched, who was I to talk?

Calvarí, like Caracol, had a spiral track revolving doggedly up it, in this case paved with polished blocks of stone. But it also had a straight, stepped way in the same glossy limestone, reminiscent of the steps up a ziggurat. At the top was a congested, tawny, neo-Churrigueresque chapel, resembling a cave in the sandstone turned inside-out and plastered impasto onto a plain Romanesque armature, not for the sake of a mannered and congealed plateresque beauty, reminiscent of used brandy snaps and prescient of Gaudí, so much as, in the manner of the manic hand-washing of an obsessive-compulsive Lady Macbeth, to shrive the architect's psyche and soothe a troubled, grandiose spirit—as is perhaps the case with every art. It had a confusing layout, so that if you went in the front you found yourself coming out the side, as with a Klein bottle or scholasticism.

Hidden behind this was the necropolis, crammed, due to space-constraints, with high-rise marble pigeonholes for human relics, amongst them, as I guessed on a ramble on that long night, those of Marla's Bavarian grandparents, *Freiherr und Freiin von Fünke. So: Marla Fünke! I loved it! And in the distance, down on the plain, was the local cement works whose tall chimneys, to snatches of clanking and screeching, and whining and hooting, perpetually manufactured cloud. And this very cloud was generating a glorious display, enticing all sorts of shades of brown, mauve, violet and purple to stream over the horizon from an invisible but still sinking sun.

Mountains iced with snow lay beyond. Jagged and improbably steep, one pierced with a hole, they had gone the most intense, singing blue in the dusk. The world itself was purple. Some trick of the sinking sunlight, the cement-works' clouds, the violet mountains.

Some things can only be said with bad taste. So if you confine yourself to good taste, you can't say them. And this has been carefully noted by those who don't want some things said, and who accordingly shift the levers of taste. Elated by fasting and involuntary purging, I was harried by such arcane ideas all through the cooling night. Sometimes I felt mad. Not cross, just insane. There was a quite unexpected rain storm, and that powerful scent of sweet-home from the dusty earth on which rain is falling. No thunder, just heavy, drenching rain falling on and on, silent but for a clattering on leaves, and a *noise* of braiding cataracts through the flume-like sand-drifts in the streets of the town below me, which reached me even here, at the top of Calvarí. I hid under the fig tree, which let only the finest, mist-like droplets through. And then the evolving scent, after a while, beneath the fig, was how fell earth as a beast would smell, if it had been running when drenched.

In the end, the rain stopped.

It was a species of arboretum up here. There was a plane tree with scabbed bark and green fruits hanging down in pairs like furry ping-pong balls. Which summoned that ancient mystery, to be faced, unanswerably, by each—which testicle did we emerge from—the left or right? And yet, so what? Or worse than so what—mystery deflowered without any advance of knowledge.

The cypress she'd meant us to meet at had tight rigid cones, like wooden Christmas decorations. Around it a bench had been built in the same glossy limestone. And on cypress bark and on the seat of the bench, her friend Jesús had sprayed a silver heart, a silver arrow, twenty silver Ms, and nine Js. There was nowhere to sit without sitting on them.

Evening done with, now it was night. There were so many cranes with red lights on them that it looked, in one part of the sky, as if the stars, flushing, had gone red. But it was only preparations for the construction of Papá's *urbanización.*

I felt a throb of chemical remorse that we could not simply have been together but had to get mashed too. It was as if a frenzy was needed, a hypertrophied communion, an Eleusis. The comparative advantages of trade, the whole being greater than its parts, the benefits of those with two right socks pooling their resources with those who have two left, by which I mean a mutual fusile ecstasy—why was this, the best buzz of all, still too meagre a buzz? We are scared to blow it so we blow it, blowing it being less painful than fear.

Marla never showed. Clearly too good to be true, if too true to be good. I feared my anxious, self-conscious passion had created a force-field of anguish she couldn't pierce. She was deffo with Jesús. *Knowing* she was, the little *shite,* as she would have put it, I felt the same fierce grass-fires flaring up in the backs of my eyes as, yesterday, had flared in hers.

Somebody asks whether it is an accident that the personage who could enchant you makes you gibber, rendering any reasonable relation improbable, precisely so you stay free. I was livid and ashamed, smarting at all levels. Melodramatic, considering we'd first met last night. Being with her only once had been like being with her in mono, but despite this she had her way of transmitting her various excitements, and making the hidden insides of all *things* thump & burn. I was hung-over, and still a little drunk. Empty, having eaten nothing; fasting, shriven, purged, exultant. In the ecstatic and mystical state of a desert mother, as well as deflated and wounded, stood-up.

Drawing a needle through a loop of its own black thread, and pulling tight. The world was becoming so dark and remorse-laden that it seemed that I had slipped down into a parallel underworld, like swimming under ice. It was now the tail-end of the night—what kind of tail is never specified, nor what lies just beneath it. I like to imagine dog.

Because something about her hadn't made sense, and it was this which drew me to her with hopeless force—perhaps just the collision in the sources of her soul between architecture and exotic dancing, between Lancashire and Bavaria. Because beneath her fizzling acceleration was a flatness, a sadness, a gloom, a misery, which the fizzle was designed to sublimate—even a terror at the condition, perceptible to anyone honest and smart, in which we wake to find ourselves. The world is a tumbril, but the crowds throw flowers. She was into flowers. And a good catch.

After the rain was done, the air smelt still more powerfully of fig. Some stiff yellow fig-leaves lay scattered about the fig-tree's roots, which clasped the rocks like veins a muscle. Beside and a little behind it, was a tree with green flowers the size of Brussels sprouts, but yellowed, as when sprouts start to rot.

Had we fucked? Last night I mean. What difference did it make? I was going in circles, and yet the question bugged me. Sadly, the devil only knew, as I have said. And why say *sadly* if I didn't remember anyway—how can that be sad? Except these balsa or even ping-pong balls. Blown eggs, even. I lurked on *Calvarí* until the sun came, emitting its fanned blue-brown rays—between heroic grape-like bunches of cloud streaming up from the cement works—the sun itself touching the bark of the cypress with jets of light, gilding silver Ms & Js, and even gilding (I sensed) my eyes. Keeping watch, convinced she wouldn't show because she was with her Jesús where she belonged, but seeing every variety of car and lorry clank or whirr remorselessly down the coast-highway far beneath me, their miniature eye-like lights still ablaze by sunlight. Even a convoy of police cars, twinkling their blue and red bulbs and making feeble ghost-train whoops, followed by a fire-engine playing the attenuated jingle, beneath the nearer scraping of jaded crickets, of an ice-cream van. And, beyond a wood of pipe-cleaner pines, was a car I'd owned in a former life, awash, and an ant-like figure, ululating presumably, and presumably fleeced, dashing in circles in the surf, and jabbing his exuberant air-guitar at bombing gulls.

Now he was doing his stomping, splashing and revolving dance, naturally enough, in a small pond on the roof of my car, which had buckled under his motion. And *now*—he was making and holding successive balletic poses, though his physique was more that of a weightlifter, fleeced as it was with whorls of lightless hair. Under a divine sun—a sun whose heat had weight, could press you down—the same sun that shone, as they embarked for Troy or Carthage—on Agamemnon, Menelaus, Aeneas.

I'd thought he was dancing, in his own emphatic way, fleeced as he was, but I have come to believe that, like God herself, he was just stomping sea-slugs. What angering words they could, in their defiance, spell on the crumped roof of the car—like those the stars combined across their aeons to shine at *us*, their sole witnesses—which as he moved about would pop out again, presumably, with a satisfying low clonk. The roof, not the worms unfortunately, nor the stars.

I had glimpsed him, I now remembered, in the hypermarket before all this, wearing his sheepskin bootees and a sheepskin hat, muted, submissive, together with sheepskin trunks—perhaps they wouldn't let him in without. The sheepskin a flaming brown, like his beard—I should have mentioned that. He'd clearly blown his mind on one of the psychotic substances circulating here off-season—maybe the substance in question was Marla herself. This my supposition, based on all that I wanted was to pound the sands, wearing knee-socks of ringletted surf, and climb on the roof of the end of the world to stomp slugs.

And only while wanting, requiring her, *some* lady, *and* some—wild, driven, with that sweet smashing smell in her hair of horse or gerbil, did I realise who the naked worm-stomper must really have been. Inarticulate; muscular; like her, driven—and this led me to understand, too, my mouth opening and a stupid look in my eyes, who she was, too, though I've since forgotten. Only I could now see, looking down from my reflective heights, that sunlight had reached the top of the shutters of Marlita's Bar. When the shutters clattered up, I went down to have it out with her.

Outside the bar was parked a stainless-steel trolley with a vat filled with boiling urine, into which a monolithic, grim woman with chalky, red skin and a dusty black bun piped cream from a *Mister Softee* machine. Some things are inexplicable.

—*¿Churros?* she asked me, her instant smile radiant.
—*No gracias.*

And she shot me the dirtiest look.

The sea outside the bar, was unable to stop heaving, and sloshing about, with something of Marla's antsiness. First thing, it had seemed just about to have a sun erupt like a missile from underneath its glittering breakers, they were such a pale and jubilant turquoise, but by lunchtime they had gone a shattered and glinting black. The shingle, rolled by the waves. And the boats which, by bubbling poisoned exhaust up through sea water, managed to make even a diesel engine sound sweet. And the slap of steel-wire rigging on aluminium masts. These not only spoke to me of Marla, but were her.

In the bar, hoping to find her, but ideally not Jesús, I drank a hot milk plus an *espresso* and fed a spiral *ensaimada* into my mouth with some complacency, though still drained and listless. The fit of the jacket, though easing with wear, was such that it was hard to get my hand to my mouth.

Followed by *chocolate con churros.* The new animation and *tendresse* of the lady with the boiling urine vat.

I waited all day for Marla, just as I had waited all night. Hanging around. Lurking. Wearing my upside down cardigan, viridian, I suppose you might call the colour, unless it was lettuce, depending on the light, carefully buttoned up, yet with a daring void in the crotch where the neck-hole was—I can recommend it, it being *outré,* like wearing chaps and nothing else. And my soft-weave tweed jacket with leather rims round the ends of the arms, and chunky malachite buttons, loaned from Marla. Beneath it, as beneath the cardy, I was admittedly naked, though very clean, inside and out. In the bar they soon got used to me, even found it in themselves, when things were slow, to interrupt their shocked, smug, whispering gossip to laugh and imitate me.

In the human interest section of the evening paper, under the words *Espectacular Accidente,* and a subtitle *la espectacularidad del siniestro,* the mysterious, grainy photo of a car hanging fruit-like in a pine. Two lovers had in their passion forgotten to apply the hand-brake. Their red *Cinquecento* had glided silently backwards, crossing camber & berm to topple off a raw shallow cliff and into the splintering crown. One of whose splinters had pierced them both.

—They are saying she was still alive in the morning, a blubbery man with a paper-white face was saying across the bar. When they pulled out the branch, *pues, kaput!* And he raised his arms suddenly, causing the silver buckle on his leather jacket to jangle. *Entrückt von den Göttern.* Txutxo too! And he hissed as if he'd burnt his mouth.

His words smelt bad, like breath. Words in general smelt good in her mouth, I had noticed, and now bad in his. Like the universe itself, it made no sense.

—¿Cerveza? he was asking. Die young, stay pretty, he said. But she left the bar a right tip. *¿Bocadillo?* As behind his head, her loopy script on the mirror, crawling like sea-slugs, instead of *Bocadillo* now spelled *¡Mad, Mental!* Except, he went on, *menos linda,* not so pretty, after that!

Marla never came. The café terrace was drifted in beds of faintly smoking sand, and I lay down and sicked-up a marmalade type of substance, from too many beers, or else not enough. The gritty brilliance of the sky and sea. Pearlescent sand-fleas, quivering, quickly formed an opalescent pool in the exact shape of the reddish, gruelly chyme, gleaming like the layer of molten wax you use to seal jam. On the surface of this molten pool were whirling patterns of dross, weather systems almost, so that I could see there the surface of a silver-green planet, and for a moment nothing else.

I rested my cheek in the gentle sand, watched the bugs enjoying their brief lives with a sedulous tenacity, my poached eye as big as their moon. I could hear Marla singing to me, though whether now or last night I couldn't have said with certainty, of joys, and endeavour.

This plump insectile pumping & trembling in setting candle-wax on the sand beneath my eyes was the most beautiful thing in the world after Marla's spirit, greenish skin, tongue. Her bare legs murky within manky jeans too big around the waist and torn out at the knees, her long bare feet, with finger-like toes, clawing at the shingle under shallow ripples. Or compressed in scuffed and bright-green bovver-boots with beaver-skin cuffs, sewn on with a bradawl & catgut in her own bedroom by her.

I noticed the swarm of bugs was the colour and lustre of semen. And could not help sampling one or two of them, just as a monkey tastes—

raising its face and dropping its hand delicately to its letterbox lips in the gesture of someone kissing bunched fingers—a louse it has picked from the scalp of its child.

Rolling on my face so as to imprint a texture on my skin, I had it in me even to sample sand. Carrots, I remembered, casting sand in my hair, are buried in dry sand to keep them fresh.

My sandy face naked or bald, but rimmed with fur, I rose and shambling across the brittle tide-marks, washed out my mouth with sea. The water very still, but swollen, not flat, as if everything was going on beneath, and ribbed like scar tissue, and faintly marbled like meat. And, too, the mounds of coloured shells—the sea sorts its shells by colour.

The air now cold in the brittle sunlight of evening. My legs lost all rigidity as if I was about to ejaculate. I lay down again for a moment on the sand-strewn street. One or two cars hooting like the geese they are, or reversing at high speed about me. Odd. What more had it been than a drunken feast with an unreliable if unbelievable girl. Who stood me up! She stood me up! With *Jesús*, the little *shite*.

Lying on my back, tears pooling in *my* eyeholes now, so that it was as if I was looking up at chunky silvered surfaces from the sand of the bed of the sea. But who could I be crying for? I was crying for me!

Familiar, yet morally enormous, she was a new kind of quality my earth hadn't had before. As an option, I mean. And I understood I'd seen her once before all this, before even the time on the seafront in the high wind, with all the grubby aluminium masts clanking their wires, and the spurts of surf gobbing on the sand with the sound of knitting. All the cockerels and dogs, too, from fenced gardens emitting their shrieks. Though I couldn't remember when. Her frenetic and alluring energy, which would not allow her to settle on whether to be drunk or sober, naked or dressed, in the water or on the beach, lascivious or chaste—she wanted everything, even the things which don't go together at all, and even can't.

More sudden waves pouncing on a beach which, like a mouse, was not all there, even dumb, mineraline. And in the waves, a fond, wild hum like the light in an eye or a tooth or a wetted lip by the gleam of a distant traffic-jam, against scents of cold rain on baked earth, rotting seaweed, fermenting figs. The mystery was one of motion: how can the dust rise up and feel and walk. How can it lie down and sleep again.

And as if she'd sung from her bonfire like Dido, *Remember me! Remember me!*, blackout curtains jerkily parted and I *remembered* at last, but stop-frame, like in a disco. Holy cow! And in case you wondered, it's secret, if anything is.

I've still got her clothes—the tweed jacket, the bright green cardy.

They smell of her.

Luce & Chris

—How's Christobel?
—She's in Ibiza, she said.
—And your mother? She smiled.
—She's dead.

This was light-years away mind, in *fin de siècle* London. The summer solstice had fallen on a Sunday—it was also going to be a full moon. That doesn't happen much. I was at an all day *barbie* on the Heath (a *Klaus* as us North Londoners called it in those trigger-happy times) drinking urine-coloured wine from plastic goblets. Then I started home. Sticky, dappled, oversaturated light—of a low red sun through black leaves. The smells of privet and hot asphalt. Sycamores weeping their juices onto tacky pavements, before whirling down their showers of seeds. Clouds of midges, landmark-swarming over an abandoned newspaper, opened to the sports pages, or else the domed red lid of a *GR* pillar box. Hostile, inquisitive children on choppers.

Nearly home, and gazing vacantly at houses, I came to one which ...—my mouth opened, and I stopped. All the windows were open. The front door, open. The basement door—open. And the *Veluxes* cracked open in the roof.

A woman sat on the stoop, bare-foot in her nylons, her patent pink heels set neatly beside her. Her hair, red-setter red, like the Marquesa Casati's, and she had a daisy-chain braided in it. She was following me not with her face but her eyes. She took a swig from a bottle of red wine.

—'Well what are you waiting for,' she asked suddenly, and winked like a clown, which made her curl open the corner of her lip. 'They're out in the garden.' I saw the gleam of teeth and the gleam of gum.

—'Out in the garden?'

—'Yes.'

I climbed the few steps towards her and she rose.

—'Blood or bandages?' she asked.

—'You what?'

—'Red or white!' And she sighed loudly to signify exasperation, then wobbled her face spitefully. 'Some people are *so* bloody trying,' she said.

And as I stood there below her (on the stoop outside what must be her house) she, holding it much too high up its neck, had tilted her bottle of wine and glugged some into a cracked mad-hatter tea-cup. Holding it out, handle-first, she offered me the bluish, inky liquid.

I took it, and even drank a little, later, when I found I needed it. *Do everything which does not disgust you,* says Spinoza somewhere. I can be squeamish, and this was borderline.

"I won't offer you crisps because there aren't enough for me, even. But sample a dry-roasted peanut, perchance?' And she widened her over-made-up eyes, in hot blue and hot pink, and flashed me a face of formal and jaded surprise.

—'In there, down in the garden,' she added in an impatient undertone, already done with me. Behind me more people were coming. 'Come in, come in, welcome,' she said holding wine and peanuts wide. 'They're in the garden.' And so on.

I was never to see her again. Yet, at least.

At the back of the house was a dim room with a bed, and beside it a mound of coats. It was the kind of a shape, organic like an anthill, unstable, that you so rarely see in cities, let alone in a bedroom. With the saturated sunlight beaming through planes of jittering dust onto its patchworked textures, I found it mesmerising.

Below the open window, down at basement-level, the garden was rammed with people. From it came a confused grumble of talk, a catalogue of laughters, a halting and bloodless music.

—'How do you know the Leakeys?' a voice from the gloom asked suddenly, as if the coat-mound itself had spoken.

—'You scared me!'

—'Answer me!'

—'But I didn't hear you come in.'

—'Yes, but how do you know the Leakeys?'

—'What?'

—'The Leakeys. How do you know them? *Silly!*'

Dying sunlight from the brilliant window was falling on her hair—blonde, curled, shining like a halo but with a faint vein of red running beneath the gilt, and standing out against the dim background like those illuminated halos in gold-leaf that are all you can see in the canvases, otherwise brown with votive smoke, that hang behind altars.

Spidering her free hand across the wall to find the light-switch—and a light came on.

Puckered, raspberry-coloured lips. A snub nose, and a wide bony forehead, deer-like, almost dumb, so you half expected antlers to crop out.

—'I don't,' I told her.

—'Don't what?'

—'Don't know the Leakeys, *silly*. Is this their house?'

—'Of course it is, *joke*. Not what I'm saying is a joke, you are.'

And she couldn't help laughing at her own joy. She was holding a dinted pint-mug filled with wine as dark as mine, in which froth and a few ice-cubes were floating. And then of course, her eyes—the rich blue of a heated swimming pool, which she had a way of half-closing whenever she smiled. They were unstable but inviting, endlessly shifting yet made out of something tangibly gel-like and solid. And just as the deep end of a swimming pool looks shallow, so her eyes looked shallow, their surface reflecting flickering streamers of light, but grained, also, with sparks.

I licked my lips.

—''Peckish?' she asked. 'Come with me. There's food in the kitchen.'

And because I hesitated before following her, she yanked my hand.

In the kitchen was a mouldy cylinder of raw stilton and an unripe wheel of brie. Three brittle French loaves, more dinted beer-mugs filled with stalks of celery and quartered carrots, and knives with dark pickle smeared along the haft. In the corner was a plastic dustbin smelling of *Pimms* and crusted with a floating dross of orange rinds and leaves of mint.

—'Stilton, or brie?' she asked me.

—'What?'

—'Stilton or brie, silly!'

—'Stilton. Silly.'

And she made me a *baguette* sandwich with celery fronds coming out each end. And making out that the baguette was an envelope, the celery and stilton being the message, and on the whole good news, she licked both ways along the baguette's sliced edges and sealed it carefully, lifting her eyes to my eyes and holding them there.

—'Bundle of laughs, aren't we?' she asked, suddenly shaking her head. 'But then, nobody's perfect,' she said, offering it me, and she giggled warmly. 'Bye, sweetheart, and one bit of advice, keep your lips shut. Something might fly in.'

Before I could answer, taking her beer-mug of wine, she'd left.

It took me too long to see I should follow her. She wasn't in the garden which I combed geometrically, pushing sideways through the centres of clots of concave & abnormally tall men in tired baggy suits, and plump, broody women with blue eye-liner. Such is our tendency to stereotype not others, but ourselves, that just as you have *tart and arch-bishop* parties, this was a self-selected lost-boy and motherly-prospect one.

I couldn't help but picture, beneath redundant clothes, wrinkled testicles, half-descended; and teats, chewy, tough. Sometimes your mind does this to you, and there is nothing for it, except to screw up your eyes, clasp your temples, bare your teeth, and throw your head about. And howl perhaps, in pain I mean, not wolfishness.

At the opposite end of the sky from the retiring sun, the promised moon had come. It was dusk.

Inside, the house itself was decorated throughout in that cheap developers' *Esperanto* of the 1980s—*magnolia* on wood-chip. The acrylic stair-carpet was the texture of wire-wool. I found the provoking girl in the last room on the top floor, sitting cross-legged on the foot of a water-bed on which she was undulating slowly, under a dangling spherical lampshade made of translucent paper.

A water-bed was something from the nineteen seventies. So was the spherical lampshade. I don't think they have them now.

Her back against the wall at the water-bed's head, hands squeezed over-tightly between her legs, and her ankles crossed with one foot jiggling, was a second girl resembling the first. She had the same, swollen, crushed-raspberry lips and the same wide, almost stupid forehead, but her hair was dark, reddened with henna perhaps, because it also seemed to glow. Her eyes dark too, and reddened, like her hair. Her nose was thinner and turned upwards at the end, unlike her sister's nose. And her skin was finer, so you were conscious of the geology beneath. One of those rare faces which, like some dreams, offer a message, watermarked into their own scary beauty, of significance, the only difficulty being to discover what this was. She was looking out at the darkening window, as if watching something invisible there, but she must have seen me reflected in the glass because *'ya-ya-ya,'* she said, slow, tired and clear. And, still staring at the window, she raised her eyebrows, lifted her upper lip from her teeth and bit her lower lip, making an unconsciously rabbit-like face.

Weird sisters. They had the same resonant shimmer or focus-pulling in the interaction between the eyes and the lips which made you unable to look away. And the same air of naive innocence, of not knowing the value of what they were. Their faces were still the faces of children who, if they did not yet know wrong, thankfully neither knew right.

With my most awkward bedside manner, I plumped down on the end of the water-bed, setting them both oscillating involuntarily, like people quaking on a blanket-bog, which made my new sandwich-making friend stretch out her arms suddenly to brace herself, and yelp.

—'Look what the cat's done on the carpet,' she said, still undulating, though less violently now, and twisting her lip in revulsion like a flirt. 'You again?' Her voice had only one note in it, a slightly blunted note—she seemed to be reading, not speaking her lines. She sounded young.

—'Watch it, cutey,' I told her, 'I'll make it lick you up.'

She laughed happily, shook her curls and screwed up her swimming-pool eyes, which made her nose wrinkle. She had a sharp bust, and as she laughed it swung with its own momentum under her cotton shirt.

—'Go wash your face, silly boy. Then tell me your name.'

—'Jack.'

There was a pregnant pause and then—

—'Jack off!' she shouted, in the tone of someone crying *bingo!*, and giggled until she burped. 'Oops!'

—'Jack it in,' I said.

But she had narrowed her eyes and was looking at me critically.

—'I know what it is,' she said after a bit.

—'What is it?'

—'You look like a dog.'

—'Thanks.'

—'No, a sweet dog. It's the birthmark. Patch, that's a good name.' And turning her head away and looking at me sideways, she yapped excitedly.

—'Shut up,' I said firmly, but she wouldn't stop yapping. 'Silence!'

She stopped yapping, but only to get the giggles again.

—'What is it?' I asked eventually, because she was finding it hard to stop.

—'Jack—*Russell!*' she said.

—'Shut up.'

—'Jack Russell! My dear little doggy-doggy Patch.'

And leaning forwards on one hand, which sank dangerously down under her weight, her legs still lotussed, she pinched my nose between her forefinger and thumb and waggled it about, squeezing up her wanton face in an expression of malicious affection. Then she went serious on me.

—'Anyway, how old are you?'

—'About the same as you I'd guess.'

—'Pity. You look younger. I *love* younger men. So immature!' And then quietly, as if savouring something on her tongue, 'So randy!'

—'Don't count your chickens if I were you.'

—'O no? I wouldn't even count my eggs if I were *you!*' she said, squealing exuberantly on the *you.*

—'Yeah yeah,' said the other, disturbing girl in a tragic, bored voice, still looking over towards the window, her lips moving fast over white teeth and her head trembling as she spoke. 'Yet *another* creepy-crawly. Go back under your stone, mate.'

I caught a side-glimpse of opaque green eyes set far apart in a stubborn face. As she turned it slowly towards mine, in a series of small, tense jerks, I had the sinking feeling you get, quite detached, between skidding towards a tree and hitting it. The illusion that you are a spectator and what you see—a looming, rapid trunk—may be sad and interesting but in no way lethal.

She was staring at me through her eyes, her head wobbling slightly, which made me flush, and then she froze, black-cat wavering in the headlamps, one velvet paw lifted in the action of walking, frightened, yet unable to cross, as the car skids sideways to miss it and there is a cascading organic *crunch.* And tinkle. With an effort which made her gasp she twisted her shoulders abruptly out of line with her pelvis. My eyes watered and the back of my neck went cold.

—'Were you christened Jack?' her provoking sister, was asking in an automatic voice. She wasn't looking at me, but fishing around in her glass with her fingers, trying to catch the ice. I had to blink to be able to focus on her.

—'Yes.'

—'Coolio. How you spell it then?'

—*'J A C K.'*

—'O.'

—'Why, how do you think?'

—'I don't know, *silly*. That's why I asked.'

—'How do you spell yours?'

She licked her lips.

—*'C H R I S T ...'*

—'Cool! Were you christened that?'

—'Wait, no, I haven't finished yet. *O B E L*.'

—'Pretty.'

—'Lucy thinks so too. Say so Luce?'

But Lucy was looking at her lap, her face hidden under her hair. No sound came back.

—'Are you there, Luce? Lights on, curtains closed, but nobody at home,' sang Christobel. 'Lucy's my sis and I'm telling you,' she continued, looking at me and nodding significantly, 'I'll tell her if you treat me bad. Ay Luce? Lucky Luce!'

She laughed, licking each of her upper teeth with a pointed tongue as she laughed.

—'Jackie, Jackie, Jackie,' she added suddenly. 'She's got a girly name. Jackie! Hehe!'

—'Now,' she asked, getting down to business. 'What star-sign are you?'

—'Guess.'

—'Guess?'

Her voice was muffled. She was crunching melting ice-cubes.

—'Guess.'

—'Taurus.'

—'No.'

—'Pisces.'

—'No.' She thought for a while.

—'I know! Capricorn.'

—'No.'

—'Tricky. You sure its not a Capricorn?'

—'Capricorn's the sheep, isn't it?'

—'Silly!' she said lovingly.

—'I'm sure.'

She thought some more.

—'I know.'

—'What?'

—'I know what sign you are.'

—'What.'

—'Aries!'

She had stamina.

—'No.'

That set her back.

—'Cancer?'

—'No.'

—'Pisces?'

—'You've already done that.'

—'Then if it isn't Scorpio I give in.'

I shook my head.

—'You're a mystery,' she said. 'Anyone else told you that?'

—'No.'

—'A ruddy mystery! Ruddy. Ruddy-ruddy.'

Lucy sighed loudly at her own reflection. Her hair, with its seam of red glowing beneath the bay, hung down on one side, like a window with only one curtain.

—'Do you believe in the zodiac?' Christobel asked, trying to revive her own interest in the subject. Her irises flickered and rolled and even bubbled like boiling water—a boiling swimming pool—that was how it seemed. It made you giddy.

—'I don't know.'

—'I do.' She licked each of her teeth again.

—'Know or believe?'

—'What?'

—'I mean I can see that.'

—'Have you had your chart read?'

—'No.'

—'Silly boy!'

Then we sat in silence for a bit.

—'Jack-the-ripper!' she exclaimed suddenly.

—'Christobel, that isn't nice.'

—'Sorry Luce.' She was quiet for a while.

—'Have you noticed anything about my eyes,' she asked eventually, and chuckled guiltily.

—'No.'

—'No, about the colour I mean.'

—'What like?' I said, innocent.

—'Well, what it reminds you of for example.'

She smiled and stared at me unblinking, as if giving me a clue.

—'Blue?' I said.

—'I know that, silly! But people say both my eyes are the colour of sapphire.'

—'Sounds pretty.'

—'It sounds alright doesn't it?'

—'Is it true?' I asked.

—'That's what I was going to ask you. But I think it's true because I went to a jeweller's to ask. He got out his thingy ...'

—'What thingy?'

—'You know, that round black thingy they all wear in one eye, a goggle thingy, and he looked at my eye with it. 'Flawless!' he said. 'You's having me on,' I said.

Was she having *me* on? *And* the jeweller? I couldn't tell. But even when you think this, it's usually not. It's when you don't think it that they are.

—"No, quite serious, flawless,' he said. 'But not sapphire, closer to sodalite. How much are you asking, if you don't mind?' Sapphire or sodalite, what do you think, Patch? Stop,' she added quickly, before I could answer. She was offering her empty beer-mug. 'First fetch me more wine. Fetch, Patch, fetch!'

—'No.'

—'No? No? *Please!'* she said, indignant.

When I got up they both undulated even more, but out-of-sync like people on a see-saw, and with a suddenly dying intensity, damped, which spoke unexpectedly to the heart.

I had filled her glass to its brim and rose up the stairs with a slow and solemn pace, ceremoniously, and when I came in holding it before me, and reached it slowly out to her, with the air of something sacred, she lifted it with trembling hands towards her lips.

—'Jack Robinson,' she said. 'I mean, you came quick.'

Unable to tilt it, she lapped at it with her pointed tongue, gazing up at me out of her shifting eyes as she did so, and her eyes swerved guiltily once, twice, and then became fixed and held mine too long as she undulated there, lapping her wine out of a beer-mug, cross-legged on the water-bed.

—'Jack-o-lantern,' she suddenly added, between laps. Pitiless.

Lucy, still undulating too, sighed loudly at her own lap, her hair dangling forwards. But as I turned to look at her she suddenly tipped up her face and shot me such a fierce look from behind the tangled strands of hair that, without meaning to, I half-closed my eyes and turned away my face—scorched by some inner blow-torch in her gaze.

It was as if people were crowding her, invisibly to us, and they frightened and revolted her, and she drew back inside, where she was, or felt, safe. Looking out through eyes a startling green, very dark, almost black, the colour magnetic until she shut them down and leant against the wall, winded by a struggle whose subliminal shouts and screams I could just hear. I saw her breasts moving. She breathed unevenly through her lips.

—'Jack,' she asked, opening these eyes briefly—the only eyes, I noted, she would ever have. 'But can I call you Jack? Not Patch, but Jack?'

Her voice had a nasal rankness in it which sounded almost debauched; mature as well as young, like someone destined to become a mother much too soon.

—'Yep?' I waited.

—'Nothing,' she said, abrupt, defiant, hostile, and cringed, suddenly pulling her shoulders upwards, clenching her elbows to her ribcage, and hunching her neck forwards. She scrunched up her eyes, but opened her mouth as if yawning and drew her lips back from her teeth.

Her face was white but her arms were a delicious brown—perhaps she'd been sunbathing in hat or veil. Her wrists were narrow to brittleness, and she had small hands. As I watched, she closed her mouth, lowered her shoulders, and relaxed her eyes, though she still kept them shut. Her head twitched sideways on her hunched neck and her cheeks darkened. Her temple was so transparent you could see the red and mauve pipes of blood pulsing inside it.

—'Hello Luce!'

Christobel had followed my gaze to her sister, but when Lucy's eyes opened they were looking straight at mine. She slowly turned her face and only then her eyes to Christobel.

—'Hallo Chris.'

They both looked younger than their age, whatever that was, but Christobel had the pure blunt voice to match her looks while Lucy gave the impression, when she spoke, of saying much more than words—you felt you had to listen between the lines to catch what was really said. And yet when you tried to, you found nothing there.

She lifted a glass from the floor beside her, took a sip of wine, hardly a teaspoonful, swallowed it, and—immediately began to laugh.

Her eyes glittered and her whole face moved, like a heroic, unexpected crescendo in a quiet, sad piece.

But then she sank back against the headboard, her spine curled, her shoulders shrank, her lips turned down, and she shut her eyes and bent down her face as if to cry. She was shivering.

—'Guess what I feel like now?'

It was Christobel.

—'What?'

—'Among other things I mean.'

—'What?'

—'More wine!' she sang out.

And as she climbed off the bed to hunt around for the unopened bottle she was sure was in here somewhere, her figure was womanly, a neat, living shape which, although you couldn't account for how, was perfect. So perfect that it was almost disinterested in its effects—the first question you asked was how it was done, and whether it would be possible for a sculptor to recapture it. Meantime, walking with her hands on the carpet, her legs still lotussed on the waterbed, she found her bottle under the low bedside table. She was wearing a *traje de luces,* with ultra-high-waisted trousers and a tatty jacket, stiff with torn braid and sequins.

—*'Jackal!,'* she suddenly shouted.

—'And you sent me all the way down for wine,' I said.

—'Gotta make yourself useful, *jack-ass,*' she explained. 'Listen, I'll tell you a joke,' she added, and aimed me a sunlit smile which warmed my forehead and eyes.

But first she poured blue wine into my lifted mug, and topped up Lucy's glass, concentrating so as not to spill it, and her face took on an angry look. Then she settled herself back on the bed, undulating as she did so, refreshing Lucy and my undulations, each of us out of phase with the others.

—*'Why is History a bore?'* she asked, composing her features and self-consciously closing her lips over teeth which protruded very slightly.

—'We don't know. Why is history a bore?'

—*'Because it's always repeating itself.'*

And she faced the ceiling and poured wine into a budding mouth which opened like a flower to receive it, looking pointedly down at me from the ultra-suggestive edges of her eyelids as she did so.

Some of the wine went up her nose. Her cheeks bloated with liquid and a wide-eyed look of happy panic came over her face. Her hands lifted to catch her mouth before it burst. Then her lips exploded in a mist of warm wine and saliva which settled on my cheeks and in my eyes. It stung, so that I had to blink repeatedly, and tears rolled out.

—'Ahh, don't cry, honey,' she said, almost at once, and she pecked my cheek.

Then she turned to Lucy.

—'Who's that over there?' she asked, pointing at the window, and while Lucy, asking 'Where, Chris?' searched in vain for vision or intruder, Christobel lifted Lucy's glass from her numb fingers with a knowing smile and a wink at me.

—'Lucifero, porter of light. Mr Lucifer,' she said.

—'You don't even know who that is,' I said.

Christobel was nettled, wronged.

—'Yes I do. Lucy in furs. Good morning, darkness, I want to say. Loop the loop, lucy loo.'

—'Loop the loop, Chris. My dear Chris!'

—'Luce, looser, Lucifer!' said Chris.

—'Chris, Christ, Christobel! My sumptuous scrumptious crystal ball. In which—you can see the whole future, and the whole future is—cute!'

—'Yes, I can see the future. And I can read *Patch* like a book. A porno book. Eeek! Hehe!'

Lucy was playing Christobel's childish game, but she was not all there. Her eyes had gone opaque again and her face was still and matt. She could respond, but she didn't seem to understand the joke, as Christobel swallowed *her* wine without drawing breath and then, satisfied, lay back on her elbows, her legs still lotussed, and licked her lips reflectively while looking at mine. She was finding it hard to keep her eyes open. She reached over to put Lucy's wineglass and her own empty beer glass on the bedside table, unlotussed her legs, flipped on her side, laid her ear on her palm, closed down her eyes. The loud pretty music had stopped at last.

She was asleep.

Lucy's crushed-raspberry mouth was forming words.

—'Jack,' she said eventually, 'I need to talk to you.'

A flash of green as she saw that I was listening. I waited while she drew a pattern in spilt wine on the bedspread, which quaked and rolled beneath her fingers. She took in a deep breath, then let it out.

—'Yep?' I asked.

Her lips were just moving over her teeth. She looked at me doubtfully. This was happening in her eyes, in her cheeks, her teeth. She didn't speak.

Christobel was snoring.

Meanwhile, I saw Lucy had self-possession. Maybe I was projecting but she looked to me like she had a low opinion of the world, felt for television a passionate disgust and read under the covers all night. As if, understanding the nature of circumstance, she wasn't the sort to flutter about like an insect flying at a bulb. And this gave her a fragile confidence, but easily bruised. I leant forwards to hear her voice, and suddenly her head was down again and she was back to sketching random capital letters and numbers in wine on the quaking chintz, hidden behind tangled tresses which weren't glossy and smelt of lanolin.

When she looked up once more she was smiling, and the magnetism was back in her eyes. When I too smiled, her face opened. The whole cast of her looks had changed.

She breathed-in and held her breath.

—'Mostly, I don't like being drunk,' she said at last, with her slight and seductive nasal intonation, carefully swallowing each word.

She was looking at her lap again, but risked a sudden glance to see my expression.

—'You were liking it.'

—'It doesn't last.'

When she spoke she had a way of drawing you to her, as if she expected you to put your ear to her mouth so she could insert her tongue. It was because she lowered her head slightly, and looked up at you, and then spoke too quietly.

—'Tell me?'

She looked depressed.

—'Well it's I *know* you,' she said suddenly. 'We've never met, but you are crucial. Strange, isn't it, that I should tell you that?'

—'Crucial?'

—'In your eyes.'

—'My eyes crucial?'

—'I don't understand, or hope I don't, and *that's* crucial.'

I too didn't, or hoped she didn't.

—'I don't talk much, you know,' she said.

—'It figures.'

—'What?'

—'It shows.'

—'Yes,' she spoke fast. 'I know. I've been listening for years and saying nothing, like those mute babies who suddenly burst into the subjunctive or gerunds. Now, about to burst myself, I need to make headroom, let some out.'

A weakness for grammatical images.

—'And?'

—'You know, I had an impression that you were someone who'd hurt me. Sliced me to the bone.'

She winced, and I too felt a blade sink and lodge in bone.

—'That's such a heavy thing to say.'

—'Hey, I haven't finished yet. And someone for whom I feel love. In advance. A strong word, but I mean it. To describe that impression. I'm not saying I love you, so no fantasising or something.'

—'Weird. And hard not to.'

—'I know. And don't you dare.'

—'And?'

—'Shut up those leading *and?s*. They make you stupid and you're not.'

—'I mean, what more?' I was stung.

—'Well I am the one who stops the world wobbling, sees the sun comes up, makes the wind blow. You can imagine, it's a strain.'

She was stroking Christobel's sleeping curls in illustration. Then drew her finger along the lines in her own hand and looked up suddenly. 'I was frightened when I saw you. And perhaps you even felt it yourself. I recognised you. But don't know who you are.'

—'What are you doing here?'

—'Why? I mean who's asking?'

—'You seem too serious for this. And it's not exactly exciting.'

—'O!' Now she was stung.

—'No, I mean the party of course, not you and Chris.'

I waited.

—'Chris made me come. It's *easy* to get stuck. I'm stuck, but I want to let my hair down sometimes. Before I go bald.'

She smiled at me, then looked scared. She wanted to withdraw what she had said.

—'Of course I want to be happy, but first of all I wonder whether anyone is ever happy, or whether they are just faking, or maybe they don't even know themselves. And second of all I don't think I am the sort to be happy. Even if everything were to come out right, I don't know that I *could* be happy.'

—'Why?'

—'Just—too sad! Drowning in air,' she said several times, 'that's how it feels, just drowning in air.'

But she smiled. Speaking urgently—there was much to put across. And yet, with moving effect, there was also the veiled playfulness in her speech of someone feigning pains in sexy if psychic places, and leading your hand to feel for them.

—'Isn't Christobel happy?'

—'Christobel is sleeping.'

We looked at her, slumped across the corner of the water-bed, snoring no more, but half-voicing animal calls as she dreamed.

—'It's true.'

—'No,' said Lucy, 'I mean really sleeping.' She drew her finger around the rim of her glass, which she'd reclaimed from the bedside table.

—'I know you mean really sleeping.'

—'Christobel isn't happy or sad.'

Christobel suddenly twitched a leg, then drew up her knees.

—'Christobel lives so much in the present that she's in bed with it. She's healthy, there's flesh on her ribs, she don't care. She's already forgotten what she did yesterday and who with, and as for tomorrow, she's not bothered, not yet. She's got no idea of time. She's a lovely, angelic animal. Drunk on life, she lives, it's all she's good for.'

Her glass emitted a shriek and Lucy snatched her finger away. A flap of wine came out of the glass and pooled in the chintz around her.

—'All?'

—'Yes, there's more than that.' She looked up again and smiled. 'Much,' she said, and her smile interfered with the axes of her eyes, making them cross a little.

—'How do you know?'

Her smile fell.

—'I don't. Why can't you say something now.'

She was trembling.

—'I can't think of anything.'

—'Rubbish. Tell me something nice. Tell me your dream, say. Unless you have a dream, I'm not interested.'

Her irises glowed with enthusiasm as she spoke, not as bright, of course, but with the shade of green of sunlight shining through a torn leaf.

—'Go on, open up,' she said, encouragingly, when I said nothing.

—'I don't like talking about dreams.'

Lucy licked her finger and marked on an imaginary blackboard a score.

—'Very good,' she said. 'One right answer, if a little cloying, if artificial-sweetener sweet. Dreams are that which you don't talk about. *I dream as I live—alone!*

She thought for a moment.

—'Then tell me something else.'

—'Like what?'

—'When you get up.'

—'In the morning?'

—'Yes, in the morning.'

—'In the morning!'

—'Is that an under-estimate? Okay, lazy bones. Then you clean your teeth and brush your hair, possibly. We'll give you the benefit of the doubt. But then,' she widened her eyes and lowered her voice so that the words resonated inside her nose, 'what then?' She was smiling at me.

—'Go to the *caff* usually, and look at the paper.' She frowned.

—'You're hiding something!' And she smiled. 'Anyways, tell me, what paper might that be?'

—'Sometimes I even read a book.'

—'Even.'

—'Or look at it, at least. Then I get impatient. So I sit there, eating toast, or looking at it, at least, but of course there is something wrong somewhere. Something left out. I know I don't have it but I don't know what.'

—'I like it!' she said, widening her eyes. The sunlight glowed through the torn leaf. She had hardly waited for me to stop before speaking. 'Mine too,' she added quickly. 'Something moving behind the bellying curtain, I can see its shape, but I hug the curtain where I thought it was and it's just a soft wind blowing in. I still can't find out what's gone missing. What's wrong.'

She was leaning towards me. Her breath smelt good. Yet it was hard to focus on her face because we were out of phase. When she rose, gently enough, I gently sank, and *vice versa*.

—'I look round the room,' and she looked around the room, making her eyes and teeth protrude, 'peer behind the curtain and see people scattered about, playing *Frisbee*, and sitting in the grass with their erotic, over-weight legs splayed out in front of them. I watch through the panes of glass—from outside only a dim face behind the reflections of the flabby clouds—and then sunlight floods in. I see Mammy coming along the pavement with her bag, and I'm in my bedroom, at home.'

—'Yes,' I said, and she leant her back against the upholstered head of the bed, breathless, undulating, and looked at me, briefly critical.

—'And that,' she summed up, 'is how my life is.'

And paused. But leant forwards restlessly, and wriggled her pelvis abruptly on the undulating chintz, as if it were a toppling *Lilo*, besieged by jelly-fish.

—'Lost, in daylight, at home, in your bedroom, with no hope of being found again. Added in is the delight of being in a strange place, and seeing it clearly for the first time. There is a wish to explore, early in the morning, when you first wake up, while the air is cold.'

Beside her, Christobel snorted, chuckled, and rolled onto her other side, sucking her thumb. Lucy cleared the gold curls away from her closed eyes and stroked her head.

—'Mm-eh,' whispered Christobel through dreams.

—'Want some more?' I asked Lucy, offering the wine.

—'Yes,' said Lucy with a brittle look in her eye, 'I want more wine. Until wine flows out through my nose like cigarette-smoke.'

She stopped, suddenly apprehensive.

—'Have I gone too far? I go too far. That's how I know I'm me.'

—'Easy does it!,' I said. But she took me seriously.

—'Easy does it, Lucy, yes.'

Some of the spilt wine which had pooled around Lucy had now flowed towards the sleeping Christobel, who was tangled beside us like a lovely murder victim. Her hair was scrubbed over her head and stuck out in wispy strands. Wine or the pressure of the bedspread had printed a pink birthmark on her cheek, so that I could just as well call *her* Patch now.

—'She *is* lovely, isn't she?' asked Lucy.

—'Lovely isn't quite it. Edible, stunning perhaps. 'Tis a pity she snores.'

—'She always snores. I just kick her and that shuts her up. I think it's important, don't you, that we should be human, i.e animal, and Christobel understands that, or I mean doesn't understand it, but is it, which is the point.'

I was filling her glass as she spoke and Lucy's fingers brushed the side of my hand. She stiffened but left them there, just touching, as if nothing had happened. Then she took them away and lifted her glass. Her teeth were white and straight, except for the canines at the side which had sharp yellow tips to them designed for tearing meat. Without this she would have been too elegant, unearthly, neutral.

—'And as for you, Lucy,' I said, 'less animal, than some erratic angel?'

—'... with broken wings, trailing them through mud. In the rain ...'

—'I surrender.'

—'*You* surrender?'

—'Yes.'

—'You know what?' She'd run out of breath.

—'What?' But she changed her mind.

—'No, I can't say.' She had blushed.

—'Go on.' But now she was shirty.

—'I can't! Why don't you listen to me?'

She took a very deep breath, held it for a few seconds, and let it out.

Then she lifted her glass to her nose and snorted the fumes trapped in it.

—'It goes straight from your lungs into your blood,' she told me seriously. 'It's the best way.'

—'What do you know about it?'

—'This and that.' She lapped a few drops up. 'I like the taste now. A poisonous twist. A nasty suppleness.'

—'Drug.'

Lucy screwed up her face. She sighed and spelt this out:

—'Alcohol childifies. The debauch is the child's joy, the hangover her illness. The trouble with drugs is you pay for them. If you didn't pay, they wouldn't be drugs.'

—'So?'

—'It's all miserable, like biting on a stone. Sweetness quickly turns to pain, and by a rule, not some random way. Every pleasure contains its correspondent pain.'

—'Correspondent pain! Like a pen-pal!'

Lucy gave me a dirty look and a formal smile which suddenly dropped, and went on.

—'And that is only the temporary misery. Behind it lies the eternal misery. It poisons us!'

I had a sense of her cringing inside. She hated what she said and hated what she did. Bitterly. But then she accepted it, arched her back, spread her arms, lifted her shoulders with her arms made into chicken-wings, yawned and, when she saw me studying her, darted out her tongue at me.

—'How?' I asked.

—'How what?'

—'How it poisons you?'

—'Fucking cruel!'

—'Tell me!'

—'When you see the shabbiness of the props and the framing holding up the sets, and the blank faces with lips and eyes painted in with *kohl* and lipstick, and the greying knickers and the greying bra, like a tangled jellyfish on the bathroom floor. Then sugar turns sour on the arch of your tongue with a chemical after-taste which lingers all day long. That's how. I'm waiting for help and it's already too late. Waiting, you don't live, you wait. But I've not answered the question. It'd take too long. I'll tell you next time.'

Then in a lower voice she added—

—'If there is one. Almost never is.'

Her skull was almost naked. You could see the pure swing of her bones under the skin. I looked at her face as she was speaking and felt my spirit shift. She stroked my lungs, palped my liver. Rearrangements were made and a balance altered. It made me light-headed and feeble, close to sick.

—'How is it poisoning?'

She laughed.

—'Stubborn,' she said, and began to draw a finger dipped in wine down my forehead and the bridge of my nose. But almost immediately she changed her mind and took it away. 'My life's been turned in on itself. It's fermenting, rank, churning, visions, fears, lusts, all in a black plastic dustbin like *Pimms*. It's not healthy.'

Her face was capable of telling the truth and expressing that it was the truth, and all with a kind of twisted, resonating loveliness, not edible, in her case, so much as drinkable. And yet stuck, as she herself put it.

—'You're marooned,' I said.

—'Mar-oooned,' she howled, like a wolf.

—'You'll need a bridge.'

—'Or a raft. I'd settle for that. But even then, the raft'd sink. Have you heard,' she added, 'how the music's stopped.' The house was silent and dead. 'Party's over.' Her lips turned down as if she was going to cry. 'We have to go home.'

—'Time to go,' she whispered in Christobel's ear. 'Beddy-byes. The flowers and animals are going to sleep.' She kissed her ear. 'How shall we wake her?'

—'Try tickling?'

Christobel drew her lips back, showing her teeth which were stained by the wine she'd drunk, but her eyes were shut. She wriggled her hard belly about, gripping her elbows to her sides in self-defence.

—'Luce' she cried, in a firm, unstable voice. 'Leave off, you're worse than Bertles. Heel! Sit! Drop! Give!'

But eventually she opened her eyes, and the pool-blue flared out from under her lids. I took her two hands and pulled her upright as the water-bed beneath us sloshed and kicked like a fetus. Then she pressed her body against mine, peering round. 'Where are we, Luce?' she asked. She looked up and tried to focus on me. 'Yuk, who's he?'

—'How are you getting home, Lucy?

—'Taxi I suppose. We live way beyond the jaded, shattered realm of the night-bus.'

—'Let's find one then.'

It was not yet dawn, but the sky was turning blue, tinged around the edges with violet, crocus and pink. It was cold, but our luck held—a black cab came almost immediately, rumbling cozy up the street, its beacon glowing. The driver swore through his window at Christobel, swaying with closed eyes and a dangling jaw, and with a yelp of rubber on tarmac, accelerated off.

—'Fucking shit bastard I hate you,' shouted Christobel, and burped pointedly, her eyes still closed.

When she deigned to open them again, we started walking. Apart from Chistobel's breath, the air smelt vaguely of hay and flowers. We passed under limes wrapped up in bundles of creepers, the pavement tacky under our feet. Christobel was the first to speak.

—'Look at the moon,' she said, and she crossed herself and spat. 'I love the harvest moon.'

—'Get your eyes tested, Chris,' said Lucy.

—'What is it then, the sun?'

—'It's a clock which says half-past three.'

—'I didn't say it was the moon,' said Christobel after a pause.

—'Yes you did.'

—'I said I loved the moon.'

—'You said look at the moon.'

—'No I didn't.'

—'You did.'

Eventually a man in a chipped *Escort* wound down his window and whispered 'mini-cab?'

The door squeaked like a coffin-lid. Christobel lodged in the middle of the seat. Lucy squeezed after her, closed the door, wound down the window and then looked up at me.

—'How will I find you?' I asked her.

—'I don't know if its a good idea' she said slowly, as if trying to work it out. Christobel had been singing, but she stopped.

—'Where's Patch,' she asked in a voice of slurred outrage. 'I'm not going without Patch.'

Lucy laughed, then suddenly cringed and bent her face down, hiding it in her lap. She twisted her neck to look up at me, suddenly.

—'I don't think you'd better though.'

—'I'll see you home at least.'

—'It isn't possible.' She smiled sadly. 'We live miles away.'

—'Come on Patch, come in this side if the old hag won't let you in.'

Christobel had opened the far door.

—'Watch the other traffic,' warned the driver.

—'What traffic? There isn't none.'

—'Christobel, shut the door please.'

Somewhere further up the street, invisible, a drunken woman was singing *Rule, Brittania!* with Victorian gusto. The red-headed woman with the pink heels and the pink tulle prom dress from the stoop, perhaps, who had first invited me in and I was never to see again, yet.

—'No.'

—'Shut the door.'

—'It is shut.'

But it wasn't. Now we saw the singer, pushing a supermarket trolley like a pram, wearing a furled plastic bag as a hat and two plastic bags bound on her feet with string.

—*'... never never never, will, be, slaves ... !'*

The song faded out as she went on down the street.

—'Okay,' said Lucy suddenly.

—'Goody!' said Christobel.

—'But only if we are quiet, okay?'

—'Okay.'

—'Okay.'

—'But *quiet*.'

—'Okay.'

—'Okay.'

And I climbed in through Christobel's open door.

We flowed down long, tatty streets, where low shops had been built over the front gardens of Georgian villas. The shop-fronts were lit here and there by the glow, neon through thick yellow *Perspex*, of the sign above a kebab shop, or a video-rentals, or else the slowly revolving bulb of a mini-cab place. It was a trip through a labyrinth, and Christobel took my hand with a grave expression and began to suck my fingers one by one.

—'Is it far?' I asked them several times.

Lucy was silent, looking out of her window, but Christobel removed a finger from her mouth to answer.

—'Very.'

—'Outside London?'

—'Nearly but not quite.'

We rolled into Parliament Square from an unexpected angle, and stirred up an orgy of pigeons feeding on Whitehall. I saw the soft white down in their wing-pits. Stone coloured birds, like details, adorned the cornices of grandiose buildings, and a statue of a man wore a pigeon cockade in its hat.

A bridge leaped a shiny river, pink one side, the other black. Beyond, we idled, as deserted traffic-lights cycled through tan, scarlet, to green. And then changed-down to climb unknown High Streets into the southern uplands of the city. Only to roll easily over into the valleys of fossil rivers reduced now to a gurgle and a flush from cast street-gratings. We sprayed through long, deep puddles in mysterious, old-fashioned suburbs, lined with decaying department stores and forgotten greengrocers, pet-shops and ornamental pubs, while through our open windows came breaths of honeysuckle and lilac. Tall houses half-engulfed in the froth of overgrown gardens, sometimes with a single top-floor light, loomed up in succession and spoke of the naughty-nineties, of suburban lyricisms, of the profound and hidden happinesses of the elderly.

At last, indicator clicking and engine rumbling, we circled a common, crowded with trees, and pulled up in a place without street-lamps. It was a dead-end, gardens bursting with weed-like sycamores and festering shrubs, with tall, dreary Edwardian houses hidden in the foliage. The smell of wet, mown grass, blew across from the common.

Christobel opened a rickety wooden gate through which a little vine had woven its shoots, and shook the trunk of an elderflower tree as Lucy and I passed underneath, showering us with plump drops.

—'Shush!' said Lucy, as Christobel laughed happily in her pure, blunt voice.

Behind a red front door, beyond a plantation of sunflowers, a dog was woofing distrustfully. Lucy pressed her key into the lock and the door swung to reveal him sagging there in his moth-eaten coat.

—'He's blind,' said husky Christobel, blowing alcohol fumes in my ear, 'and he smells. I can't forgive you, Bertie, you're smelly,' she told him, taking his bleached muzzle in one hand and tapping him on his dry muzzle. 'Bertles, Bertikins, you miserable hound, smelly, smelly!'

Bertie's tail wagged on in weariness.

—'Shush!' repeated Lucy sharply, and she was serious.

A flash-bulb went off repeatedly in the air before our eyes. That was the effect. And I seemed to be receiving cackling bursts of agonising radiation in the canals of my ears. I believed I was shouting, at exactly the pitch to make my lungs and my skull-pan resonate. When I touched it, my scalp was wet. But I had my mouth shut. It wasn't me.

Christobel, her eyes down, was laughing, hiccupping, laughing. Lucy, eyes tense and mouth swollen but closed, was looking up the stairs. When the vibration stopped, with the abruptness of the supernatural, we had been transfigured—I had the shaken-up all-wrong sense of having been plucked to a different place. The silence itself was burring and ringing, and in it Christobel spoke.

—'It's only Mammy,' she said. 'She gets like this.'

Upstairs the screamer, out of breath, was frothing up the air in her windpipe. I heard her inflate her lungs again, until strung, and then the rich, horrid, shrilling voice—monotonous, mature, psycho-active, with a high whistle of terror and a lower buzz of contentment, shriek again on the same dumb note, erring on the side of flat.

Again, abruptly, it stopped.

Bertie looked up at me and swung his tail in friendly shame.

A gilt and marble sideboard in the hall, was adorned with earthenware pots of dead flowers.

—'It's just Mammy,' said Christobel again.

—'Yup,' assented Lucy bitterly.

—'The flowers I mean,' said Christobel. 'The window boxes, the pot plants. Luckily she always runs out just before she gets the sunflowers out front.'

—'Tipping up the kettle,' said Lucy, 'with a look of naughty glee which turns to hammy disappointment when only a few last steaming drops come out.'

Lucy was trying to make the best of it but her face, as she spoke, despite her matter-of-fact remarks, was pulled tight against her skull from all around her hairline. She made a noise like a chuckle or cough. We waited.

—'Lucille?' came down in a manly voice. 'Is that you?'

And when Lucy failed to answer, the manly voice in a state of wonder said—

—'I put boiling water on all the flowers.'

Lucy again failed to answer, and slowing steadily like a car alarm whose battery is running out—

'Lucille, Lucille, Lucille, LuCylu, Cylu, ... ?'

A bowl or vase crumped meekly on carpet, and after a pause an orange jumped lazily down the stairs.

—'Bounce, bounce, bounce,' said Christobel, following its reluctant, halting passage with her face.

The screaming started up again. All kinds of dreary tones crept in. It had the fuller timbre now of late Romantic opera. You could hear the resonance of mildewed lights, a tambourine sizzle amidst soggy chords, and flapping screamers of music floating up through clenched, brownish pegs. Lucy turned her tightened face to me. Her cheeks were wet.

—'I want you to listen to me Jack. I'm serious.' And she laced her hands round the back of my neck and jerked my face to hers, harshly, as if to kiss. She was looking back and forth between my different eyes. 'Watch out about Christobel. You understand me, Jack?'

But Christobel had already got hold of one of my hands.

—'Come on, Patch,' she was saying, and she began to pull at it. Lucy was still speaking.

—'Only so many people in the world. They can't be wasted.'

—'Come on Patch,' said Christobel, and tugged suddenly. I lost my balance and had to take a few steps back. Lucy followed, holding my neck.

—'Understand what I am saying, Jack?'

—'Know what Luce, just remember I *found* him! I'm asking you!'

—'Jack?" Lucy asked me again.

—'Come on Patch.'

But Lucy watched her words sink in. A sonic, hollow boom on the floor above us was followed, at long last, by the needling sound of shivering glass. Lucy stooped like a ballboy to scoop up the orange and scampered up the stairs.

—'Oh Lucille!' we heard. The manly voice had dropped to a theatrical whisper. 'But only you know, only you my love know where they are, in the cupboard I pushed it over!, behind the curtain I ripped it down!, in the fruit, I squished it like a *bug*!, oh my!'

She started gasping.

—'Alright Mammy, I'm here now.'

—'But Lucille, I ... Oh baby, its so *bloody*. They whisper Lucille, Jesus Christ, they shout. In the blind, right there. Lucille. But what was that?'

—'Alright Mammy, I'm here, I'm here.'

—'Shush Lucille will you please, I'm trying to listen!'

—'Relax Mammy, I'm looking after you.'

—'But how *dare* they. Bloody gossips. O boy, I'll kill them, the blinking pervs.'

—'Come *on*, Patch,' said Christobel with sleepy petulance, and she stamped her foot. As we listened I had been following her slowly, pulled by the hand, towards a hall table on which were a white telephone, a beaten-copper dish of coins and keys, a single sheepskin glove, and a plate of rotting food, furred-up with a blue moss which no-one, not even Bertie, wanted to eat. Beside the telephone was a cupboard door, under the stairs. Inside, mysterious steps led down. I leaned back to avoid the inverted treads of the staircase above as we descended into a low cellar, walled with naked but varnished brick and fitted up as the girls' own flat.

There was a poster of Madonna and a poster of a very fat lady in a red bathing suit, cocking her leg and making an *O!* with her lips. There was a Pooh, an Eeyore and a folding paper duck shading the lightbulb. The carpet was laid on concrete, with no give in it, and smelt of Bertie. An old television set, of the sort that was shaped like a box, stood on splayed legs; and a corner was filled with bean-bags where you sat to watch.

—'What happened to Eeyore?' I asked.

—'Well, we used to share him.'

—'And?'

—'Luce decided she wanted him to herself.'

—'And?'

—'I wanted him too.'

—'Yes, but what happened?'

—'Can't you see?'

He'd lost his tail and his head was hanging sideways by a thin remaining ribbon of grey flesh. By the look on his face, he'd seen everything, now.

—'Luce tried to take him, but I held on.' She was shifting things about and closed the door.

—'Let's watch something now,' she said, pushing me towards the beanbags. 'Sit down there.'

And she rummaged in a heap of video-cassettes.

—'And Pooh?'

Pooh had a mournful expression, and his t-shirt was rucked up on a pregnant belly.

—'Oh, that happened after.'

—'What happened?'

—'We used to share him.'

—'And?'

—'Luce wanted him to herself.'

—'And?'

—'But can't you see? Don't you get?'

He had one arm left but no legs. Both his eyes had been pecked out and optic nerves hung loose.

—'I guess so, yes.'

—'Yes,' she said sadly. 'Yes.'

—'But she never loved him,' she added after a long pause.

—'How do you know.'

—'Judgement of Samson.'

—'Meaning what?'

—'These two women, okay, both are arguing over a baby. Well, says Samson, we'll cut him in half and you can have half each. Yes!, says one of them.' Christobel giggled. 'But the other one cries. No, give him all to her, she says. And that way Samson knows it's her telling the truth and she gets her baby back. You ought to know that, silly.'

She pressed a cassette into the video machine and began to rewind.

—'What is it?' She didn't answer, but licked her finger and drew a cross of imaginary duct-tape which sealed my lips.

—'Shush,' she said and went into the bathroom.

I waited.

Through the hollow wall I heard the mineral stream of her piss striking the toilet. She farted accidentally and the sound resonated in the depths of the toilet bowl like a low note in the bell of a euphonium. 'Oops,' I heard her say, and laugh. Then the rumble of the toilet roll on its holder, the snap of the seat as, sticking to her flattened thighs, it lifted before dropping back. Finally, the sound of swirling water as she flushed. She came back with a near-empty bottle of whiskey wedged against her chest, an unlit fag in her mouth, plus a catering pack of dry-roasted nuts.

—'We don't let Mammy down here,' she said, with eyes looking up and to the side. And plumped down neatly beside me without using her hands, by crossing her feet, crouching forward and rolling back—'Both Mammy and Bertles are barred. But Bertles is allowed in if he's good.'

Then, going on all fours to a wall-socket she started the blow-heater. And depressed a button on the telly which burst into a blizzard of crackle.

Then she settled herself near me on the beanbags and brandished the remote-control wand at the video. It clicked and whirred and the titles of a film began to roll. It was *Gone with the Wind.*

Her eyes and her teeth were glittering expectantly in the light of the screen, and she turned and smiled to me. Again I got that too-long look, subtle as a jab on the nose. Keeping her eyes on me, she sucked at the up-turned whiskey bottle and the whiskey glugged and burbled as she drank. She rubbed her hand on her lip and passed it over to me saying 'Huh?', and I drank too, and eyes on the telly now she held out the gaping peanut bag and waved it enticingly about. She turned on me again in the light of the screen, and smiled some more. Then she wriggled her bottom to settle it better amongst the beans. They made the sound of shingle.

We finished the remains of the whiskey and Christobel located a four-pack of *Special Brew.* She smiled, but looked like she was about to cry. She reached out her knuckles and stroked my cheek. Her eyes were black in this light, with the dancing gleams of a swimming-pool by night, and tilted down like her lips at the ends. It hurt me, looking at her, but it was the sort of ache you want to try over, again and again.

Her cheeks held the exaggerated promise of the female lead in a soap opera.

She was licking her lips. She ripped apart the four-pack like a bunch of fruit. 'You?' she asked as I took one. Then she pointed her tin in my face and with the gesture of someone letting off a grenade, pulled out the ring. Foam spurted and a cold sticky film settled on my cheeks and eyelids. Christobel laughed in a lazy voice, tipped back her head and drank.

I opened my *Special Brew* and drank too. I felt the cold liquid snaking its turns and twists through my winding guts. A labyrinth for beer! I too was losing my way. The world was sweet and I could taste its sweetness. My heart felt sweet. My arms and legs did too—it took all my will to stop them rising up and waving like a baby's.

She moulded a stand for her beer in the beanbag and turned towards me again. 'I think you should kiss me now,' she whispered.

—'You're feeling bold,' I whispered back.

—'Bold! I'm bold every single day of my life.' She lay on the bean-bag and closed her wanton eyes. Her lips came apart over her teeth and she put a serious expression on, trying for once to concentrate.

—'I'm waiting,' she whispered after a while. She waited.

—'Are you going to, then?' Her forehead had wrinkled and she was taking big breaths. Unless it was the unsteady light of the television, I could see her heartbeat vibrating her shirt.

—'No.'

—'Why not?' She sounded aggrieved and surprised. She waited.

—'Because.'

I didn't want to kiss her, only to bring my face up close to hers and look at her lips. I could smell the sweetened drink on her breath, and all the cigarettes she had ever smoked, which she'd somehow converted into an irresistible come-on type scent. Her lips opened a fraction wider, and she licked them because they were going dry. Now they were glossy again. They were Lucy's lips, over-ripe, swollen, rich.

Christobel's eyeballs were moving under her closed eyelids. She opened her teeth, and I saw her tongue moving behind them. I touched her lips with my finger and she started to giggle.

—'Sorry,' she said, snickering, her eyes shut tight. 'It was just something I thought of.'

—'What?'

—'Because.'

Feeling around in the dark for her tin of beer, she knocked it over. The beer foamed and sank away amongst the beans. She threatened me with another tin, and carried through her threat. Beer was dripping from my chin. Then raised her head to take a swig, and started to laugh into the tin as it dribbled down her cheek and dripped onto the front of her shirt so that one blood-gorged nipple showed through. She rolled over onto her front to laugh better and pushed off each embroidered matador pump with the toe of the other foot.

It was hot in here with the blow heater blowing, and hard to think. Something stronger than I was had got a grip on me, and I could feel myself being twisted about.

—'Does it matter?', she asked me. I couldn't answer that.

—'Does anything?', she asked.

She laughed, though not convincingly, with her face pressed into the coarse musty fabric of the beanbag. She turned it towards me and sucked at her thumb. She was staring through blinking, half-closed eyes. Your heart rushed when you looked at her face. Keeping her eyes fixed lazily on mine, she rolled onto her side, and took my hand, and held it against her damp breast.

—'Here,' she said. It was firm, like a hard-boiled egg. I hadn't expected that. She moved it to the other breast, the dry one. And then she placed it in the hot armpit between her thighs and moved it unevenly back and forth. 'And here,' she said, smiling, arching her neck, rubbing her cheek in the beans, softening me up.

She brought my hand up and kissed it, and sucked each finger slowly as she had in the mini-cab, keeping eyes like peeled blue grapes fixed on mine.

—'Does it matter?,' she asked again, so gently that I could hardly hear her. I could smell salt. Something was pulling on me, not gently at all, so that several times I'd almost lost my balance and slipped, and I felt I had to lie down quickly now in a rocking boat that was being pulled away from the shingle and out to sea. At first I couldn't make it stop, then I didn't care, then I didn't want it to.

—'Does anything?,' she whispered, and laughed softly, and there was everything sweet in her laugh. Time foreshortened and I *really* wanted to live. The future had evaporated, and the past. She shut my eyes with a finger, put her hands on my ears, and carried my face slowly on to hers. 'Kiss me properly,' she said, and I kissed.

Christobel crumpled up her face in disgust and pushed me away. She wriggled out of her matador jacket and without undoing the buttons, crossed her arms and folded her shirt over her head. Her belly swelled below the taut skin which was caught around her rib-cage like the fine cotton of a white dress, rucked a little and moving with each breath. She shook her hair in her lifted hands and caught it back behind her ears. And she smiled at me with all the innocence and all the wickedness of childhood sex. 'Kiss me really properly,' she said again, warmly and sadly. Her teeth were sharp.

With her fingers she tugged at my shirt, jerking it very slowly, inch by inch, from my trousers, and I shuddered. She weaved her fingers back and forth across my stomach, slipping them under the belt, down behind the flies. She made a ring with her fingers, and with another hand unbuttoned and unzipped.

She unclipped the side of her matador slacks and slid them down a little, and moved her pubic bone, hidden behind the smooth cotton of her underpants, to press on mine. Then she pushed me away suddenly, curling her lips in distaste.

She took the high-waisted slacks of her *traje de luces* by the black elastic tape which ran under the arch of each foot and pulled the legs over her feet, rolling the slacks into a ball and lobbing them in behind the television set. She waved her legs around like a topsy turvy spider, advertising their nakedness, their liquidity, their apartness. And, still wearing her underpants, she rolled back to me, and cleared my shirt away from my chest, and pressed her breasts slow and hard against me as if to tusk me, and hooked her leg on my hip. 'What does it matter,' she asked me softly, and again she laughed.

She lifted open the leg-hole of her underpants, which was rimmed with a frill, and scissored her pins, a girl in a yoga class. 'Patch,' she was asking, 'Patch?' She opened her eyes to kiss me again and she was smiling. Her frank, open stare made me shy. It was too close to be looked at like that. 'I want you to ...' and she gurgled.

—'What?'

—'... *Come* inside me Patch,' she whispered, all delinquent seriousness, the emphasis on the *come*, while playing some complicated trick with her hands between our legs, and then she laughed as if the trick had worked.

Each time she wriggled she caught her breath. 'I want to *see* you fucking me, Patch,' she said, somehow close to tears, her eyes now closed.

Her arms were crossed between us, as if to protect herself from me, and her head was nestled down by the side of my neck where I could feel her teeth biting softly at the skin. She moaned and began to making slurping noises, and her teeth were tugging, tightening the skin around my neck like a rope.

Speaking in retarded sounds and handling me with harshly, she screwed up her teeth to say *fuck you, fuck you, fuck* by breathing in, in a higher and higher voice. She froze in mid-sentence—her eyelids flickering, her lips darkening, eyes searching for her eyebrows—and widened her lips with scorching noises for a long yellow tongue to come out, forked and vibrating at its tip like a flame. It hung in front of her face, glossy, rigid. And fell with a padding sound in a stripe across the beans.

She sat up abruptly as from a nightmare, with longing yellow whiskers swinging and dangling from her lips. Her hand rose to her mouth. Multi-coloured gruel rolled out between her fingers and dropped.

She turned towards me in surprise, drawing her lips back over her teeth in a taut, apologetic smile. Her belly stiffened to wood and a second gush of vomit slapped the side of my throat.

She shut her teeth with a click.

She'd got it on her cheeks and her chin, and acid lumps of it were caught in the curly hair around her temples. Her eyes closed and she fell against my chest, rasping. The room filled with a sharpened, bitter stink.

When I tried to lift her, her head sagged, her knees rolled apart and her hands lay beside her, palm-up on the beans. She was sweaty and cold. In the bathroom I raised the toilet seat and propped her chin on the china toilet bowl which should almost, you felt, have a ready-made depression, like hair-salon basins, for this. I tugged the pull-switch for the neon strip-light and locked the bathroom door. Christobel was bubbling like a drain and every so often I heard her sniff. Combing her mucky fingers through her curls, and using her ears as hairclips, she tried to keep her hair from dipping in the water. She began tentatively to giggle.

—'Christobel?' asked a voice through the door.

Her giggling stopped.

The handle moved up and down, twice.

—'Chris?'

—'Don't let her in Patch,' whispered Christobel. 'O please God thank you, I beg of you, don't let her in.'

She gurgled and a few more mouthfuls of vomit splodged out.

—'Chris, where's Jack?'

—'Don't tell her. O God.'

—'Where is Jack?'

—'I'm in here,' I said.

—'No he isn't,' said Christobel quickly, then put her hand over her mouth. There was a scrap of silence outside.

—'Open the door, Jack,' said Lucy.

—'Don't let her in.'

—'Jack, open it please.'

—'Please don't, Patch. O God, please.'

But the bolt buckled on the door, the screws popped, and the door opened softly. Lucy stood in the white neon daylight, watching. The automatic extractor fan cut in.

Christobel, lifting her buttocks inside her cotton knickers, leaned further into the toilet as if to drink.

Lucy stood looking at us. Her eyelids were drawn back, her pupils very large. The eyes shone, and then the whites turned pink. The muscles in her lips went limp. She twisted up her hair into a rope and pulled it over one shoulder. The automatic fan cut out.

—'Go away, Chris,' she said quietly. 'Go in the garden, go upstairs, I don't give a fuck where you go.'

Christobel gurgled and slipped further in, as if to hide or even escape.

—'Christobel,' screeched Lucy, 'OUT before I flush you down the fucking toilet you turd.'

And she barged past me and pressed the flush lever. Christobel pulled her head out, her face wet with surprise. She whimpered, blinked, and scurried away on bent legs, holding her ears in her hands and looking at the floor. Lucy kept her eyes on me as if I too might make a break for it. We heard the sliding picture-window which gave onto their basement-level garden grating in its runnel as Christobel went out. She wasn't so much walking as dragging her legs behind her like a bridal train, her arms crossed on her breasts and squishing them. Lucy inhaled slowly, several times. She too laughed.

—'Hilarious, isn't it. You silly, fucking, *idiot.* You bloody *cunt.* I'm not referring to your disgusting lechery, it's your heart which isn't, fucking, good enough. I could've been so happy, lying beside you each night, waiting for morning to come. We could've been great together, but you were just not shitting good enough and couldn't hold it in. For nothing! Cheap little moron. She's no good to you. It's not her fault that her brain's between her legs. She'll be bored of you tomorrow. She may be lovely but you're too special for a girl without a heart. She hasn't got an idea in her exquisite head, except bonking and we all know about that, cunt. But I could've expected better of *you*.'

She took breath in a series of catches. She was waiting for me to speak, but as I opened my mouth she went on.

—'*Turd!* I thought my wait was over. So happy, at last. I've been looking since I was a little girl. And I've never *seen* you before. And look what you've gone & done to deserve it now, *prick*. Look what you've fucking done, *shit-face*. Think of those children we never had, *arsehole*. Because you won't find another fucking woman like me. I was so, so wrong. And what a bloody fucking tragedy it is, *dick*. Like dying young.'

Her eyes were wide. I could see the whole of her iris, an oxidised copper ring, surrounding glossy blackness in the centre, surrounded in turn by a ring of pinkish white. A faint concentric ring under each eye completed the circle of which her eyebrow was an arc. She had a mechanical, unrealistic look, staring around blankly at the bathroom now, at the shampoos cluttered at the end of the bath and the coiled rubber shower hose hung above it on its white plastic hook.

Her nose was running, and she licked up at it with her tongue. She was panting. She looked back to me, her green eyes clogged with sticky tears which matted her lashes like snot. Again, the sequence of flash-bulbs going off, and forking, notched lightening-bolts in mauve migrating across my sight. A stark, bitter agony just in front of each ear, under the skull, a migraine switched on and off, and then a gravelled voice saying, smoked and low, like a man's—

—'Lay into him, Lucille!'

Lucy, twisting and pulling the rope of her hair, looked frightened and shrank. Mammy was calling from the foot of the stairs.

—'Get him, Luce!'

Her human shape moved down the steps and into the range of the light cast through the bathroom door.

—'It's you?' she asked, suddenly uncertain,

Her greying face, lined like exercise paper, was punctured with seeping red eyes, but her hair, escaping from a lilac towel bound around her head, was blonde like Christobel's, only straggly and coarse. She was wearing blocky trainers with no laces, their tongues hanging out. A bath-towel, tight as a bandage, nipped the top of her breasts. She approached stiffly in small steps, her head held erect, her elbows clamped at her sides and her forearms out, dowsing her course through time and vacancy. She opened her mouth, was silent, then spoke.

—'Have you known my daughters long?' she asked, in the bright tones she might have used to say, 'Another biscuit?'

It took me a moment to answer.

—'Just met them tonight.'

—'Absolute rubbish!' Her gums were bleeding, and at the centre of her lower lip a thread of brownish spittle formed and lengthened hypnotically with a single drop at its end, like a wary spider on its thread. I had to fight not to focus on it. 'I wasn't born yesterday. I'm quite aware you've been plotting.'

—'Plotting what?'

—'Plotting *to*, not what!'

Under her hair, you could see the shape of her scalp. Her lips had the ringed texture of an earthworm. She moonwalked towards me, majestic, and taking the meat of my upper arm between two fingernails, squeezed as if crushing a bug.

—'O boy!' she said.

As I pulled my arm away her fingernails tore through a small wedge of skin. At the end of an inflamed sickle of flesh swelled a globe of orange blood.

—'Yes,' she breathed, huskily, 'oh baby, *look* what I've gone and done.'

And then in a businesslike, more nasal tone—

—'And I meant it!'

But as I backed further into the bathroom, she was marking me.

—'Didn't hurt,' I said—not helpful, just a playground reflex. But in a new tone of voice, grating, like the same actress taking several parts:

—'It's plotting *to*, not what—plotting *to* fuck my girls?'

And she suddenly raised the fingers of both hands to her bared teeth, to gnaw at them like a harmonica, or corn-on-the-cob.

—'Lucille!' she added high-toned, nasal, swinging round at Lucy who was wedged between bath and basin, the dusty wall-mirror disclosing her rapid hands plaiting the rope of bay hair behind her head. 'Isn't it heavenly? Surprise, surprise, he's back.'

And Mammy gripped the towel-rail purely to make her joints crack.

—'Who's back?' asked Lucy resignedly.

—'But, *he* is of course,' she said, making big eyes at me.

—'But Mammy, he's never been.'

—'Don't be so bloody ridiculous, Miss,' Mammy laughed, through Lucy & Chris's lips, though withered now, with scabs of red crystal clustered in the corners. They came apart over scattered brown teeth for a smile, and above the smile, a wispy mustache and Chris's nose. 'Hardly a question of having been,' she muttered, 'when he *lived* here!'

She was shaking her head in sarcastic spite. When she saw me studying her and opened her mouth and put her hand up in surprise. 'Oh!'

Then she held out bone-like arms invitingly, tilting her girlish head to the side.

—'Lover-boy,' she said sweetly at last. 'O my!' Her voice wondering, manly and droll. Without a whisper, on cue, the towel lost its purchase on the brittle skin and fell around her feet.

She had the air of an unravelled mummy.

—'How are we keeping?,' she asked.

Laps of flesh dangled here & there from her body and udders hung down her front, empty but weighted with a few uneven lumps. Madness, as it sometimes will, had aged her—the blow-torch of psychic greed! Naked except for a pair of white cotton underpants of the same brand, leg holes rimmed with a pastel-blue frill, which Christobel wore. Examining herself briefly, she looked up, radiant.

—'Lucky I've got my undies on,' she told us, furling her hands inside the waistband like a nervous child.

Her knees were slightly bent, and her back folded round the axle of her arms, so that her neck projected forwards, like the neck of a four-footed creature. Her face was tilted up from its natural ground-facing position.

—'And about time, too,' she added, in the guttural version of her voice—in an accent Dutch or Danish, perhaps, expressing irresistible spite. I *knew* you'd be back in the fucking end. Can't stay away, can you, rascal. But don't think I'll take you back. You revolt me! Filth! You make me vomit!'

Working her underpants down over her hips in a matter-of-fact way, she plonked down on the edge of the bath and sighed. 'Crawling back,' she told herself faintly. A rippling stream of piss swirled away to the plug-hole. 'O my godfathers I needed that,' she added, smiling manfully as she pulled her underpants back. 'You know who I saw darling, coming home with the shopping?' she went on, turning to Lucy with pointed inconsequence. 'Maggie Thatcher's severed head, hanging in a thorn bush by the hair. Nearby, lying on the ground, her severed hand, of a bluish tinge, all bloated like a rubber glove. It wore a wedding ring. And as I passed, know what? Maggie turned and followed me.'

—'How can a head follow you? It's not got legs' said Lucy, sullenly.

Her mother allowed her own head to tilt with good-natured exasperation.

—'Miss Lucille Compeyson—with her *eyes* of course! What did you do today? Anything fun? In the park, as well,' she went on before Lucy could answer, 'there was such an adorable doggy, wagging his little stump of a tail and having a silly half-hour with a stick. It was Bertie, when he was a puppy.'

And she offered us both a long, fixed, radiant, hostess-smile which sank like a soufflé as she buried all her fingers in it. Then covered her eyes with her hands as if counting one hundred, although I could see a dark attentive redness, glittering through the cracks.

Lucy, who had been studying me, turned suddenly with a puzzled look.

—'Mammy, why do you think it's Daddy?'

—'Because it is.'

—'No, but why do you *think* it's him?'

—'It is.'

—'Mammy! But it *isn't*.'

—'It is.'

Lucy was worried. Tilting her own head, she cleared away the tears from each eye in turn with the base of her palm. She sniffed.

—'It's a new one on me,' she told me. 'It's not Daddy, Mammy, it's a friend of ours,' she added loudly and slowly in the kind of voice used for chastising babies.

—'Isn't?'

—'No.'

—'Daddy?'

—'No.'

Their mother gasped and turned to me, her hands on the side of her head.

—'It can't be true?' she asked.

—'I don't see how!' I said.

Meanwhile, out through the picture-window, framed for us through the bathroom door and their varnished-brick romper-room, Christobel still squatted naked in the blue grass of the garden, her ringlets in rat-tails, arms crossed over her breasts. Tuned-in or led-on perhaps by Mammy's intermittent screeching, an owl which had been calling on the neighbouring common now, amazingly, was clasping an overladen branch just above Christobel's head, rotating its face, humourless & alert, robotically on a static body.

—'O it always comes,' explained Lucy, 'because Christobel feeds it the pythoness's thawed-out mice. You haven't seen the pythoness yet, she's in the kitchen. We thought he was a python but she laid an egg. She doesn't seem to care about her left-overs going to the owl. Mammy says she's depressed.'

Raising a delicate claw whilst tilting its head with a look of simian delight in its eyes, the owl scratched beneath its scruffy feathers, stained brown & white like the plumage of a chain-smoker.

—'The owl too, they're all depressed. We call him *Mope*. Unless he lays an egg.'

But speaking very fast their mother interrupted—

—'Me-me-me-me-me!'

—'Shush, Mammy,' Lucy said. And with forlorn gusto—'What good news, now you can go back to bed!'

—'O baby, I think my world's gonna fall apart,' said Mammy.

Lucy was trying to twist her mother round and push her out of the bathroom, which was really too small for three of us. The mirror had steamed-up and we were getting irritable, like people stuck in a lift.

—'You think I'm mad, don't you!', their mother said. 'Hah, he thinks *I'm* mad, huh? That's what I say to you.'

And she stuck out her tongue and corkscrewed her reddening face at me.

—'My, my!,' she added.

But then—

—'True?' she asked again in a wondering voice, leaning her weight against Lucy's hands so that Lucy had to put her shoulder to her back to prop her up.

—'Mammy, go back to your room before I smack your naughty bum,' she said severely, 'you stupid little girl.'

—'Won't!' said Mammy. And calling Lucy's bluff—'Make me!'

—'*Mammy!*' shouted Lucy. And, teeth clenched, still propping Mammy from behind with her shoulder, she used her hands to snap an imaginary chicken's neck.

—'You come to bed then too,' Mammy was saying. 'If I have to.'

—'I understand now, Lucy,' I said. 'I made a mistake. Forgive me. I want to forget everything that's happened and start again.'

—'Not possible,' I heard her say.

—'Yes it is.'

—'Is incest possible?'

—'This isn't incest.'

—'Well, it is for me. Or it would be. Chris would do it definitely, but I can't. Not possible.'

—'True?' their mother asked over her shoulder, still leaning all her weight on Lucy.

—'You can't let something imaginary like that overturn your life—or you were making out it would overturn your life,' I said.

—'It's something I can't change. It's not a choice. It's like a fact. You can't change facts.'

—'You can.'

—'Only thing I don't get is why you came back now?' asked their mother.

—'You can't.'

—'And about time too!'

—'That was Patch, I'm Jack, it wasn't me.'

Admittedly, that was a stupid to say. If I hadn't said that, it might still have been okay.

—'Well now I know you can't if you're going to say idiotic things like that.'

It felt I was under water, and could see Lucy's face and her body, bulging in unexpected ways with the quicksilver slop of the surface, and even hear her voice, but she wouldn't reach down and snatch me out.

—'Why can't you?'

—'I know I can't. I really do. It isn't something that can be changed. It's not something I can do.'

Clear water, now, was brimming in her reddened eyes.

—'Why can't you.'

—'You think I am being hard on you, like taking it out on you, but I'm not. I'm as sorry as you are, except I know there is no option, and I don't know whether that makes it worse or less.'

—'But you said it wasn't possible for me to come here,' I pointed out, 'and I did come.'

A triumph gleamed on her face, like someone who, thinking they had lost, has seen the way open up to mate in one or two moves.

—'And I was so bloody right. You shouldn't have come. Look at the fucking mess.'

From upstairs, blind Bertie woofed questioningly.

—'Lucille, get out,' said her mother, calmly, leaning against her, back to back. 'This has nothing to do with you. In the garden, upstairs, I don't care, just out.'

—'Lucy, it's pride,' I said. 'Or temper. You're not thinking straight. Nor was I.'

—'It isn't pride, it isn't temper: it isn't *possible* at all. Okay? Not possible.'

—'Out!' commanded Mammy, in a voice which rang like an organ note. 'Go Lucille, I've had enough of this.'

—'Shut up, bitch,' said Lucy.

But her mother had turned to me.

—'*God*, you've not changed. Well-preserved, aren't we! Hope you like your daughters, think them well turned-out?' She turned her face to Lucy. 'Lucille I've had enough,' she said quietly, her voice going high and melting into tears, but then it descended into a strung guttural violence to add, 'It's like this every time. He comes crawling back. But never again! *I'll* see to that!'

If the purpose of life is, before dying, to untangle the knots in your soul, she was working the other way, in raveling them up, even knitting with them, with an element of virtuosity.

—'Mammy I'm telling you, if you don't calm it and go to bed we'll put you in a home for special people.'

Mammy put on an imbecile face, raised her fingers and thumbs to her tongue, tasted the horror on their tips, and closed her lips over them.

Next, she inhaled carefully through her nose, extracting one hand to rest as lightly on the towel-rail as on the baby grand at a recital. The other she fanned delicately behind her hip. She paused, cleared her throat, opened her mouth, and screeched again. From the garden, just above Christabel's matted curls, the owl came to life & screeched back. Nothing static about him now—on his branch, he appeared to be dancing—shuffling first one way and then rapidly back.

In this bright room, whose only soft furnishings were people, towels and a bathmat, Mammy's screeching inflicted direct physical pain. I pulled my top up over my ears. But it made no difference. Lucy shook her by the shoulders, and the shaking modulated the screeches in a ludicrous way.

—'Go away now, Jack,' she shouted, turning her head back to me. 'She'll never let up otherwise, and she might go funny on us.'

—'This isn't funny?'

—'You're not helping, Jack. Go away now while there's still time. She cuts up rough.'

On those words, the screaming stopped. 'Bye-bye, boyfriend,' Lucy shouted into the unexpected silence. Then, more quietly, 'It was nice knowing you. Enjoy your little life. Remember what it could've been, and think of me when the time comes to die. Poor Jack, you'll suffer. I shouldn't be so hard on you, but it's your own fault. Most people look forever, or settle early for second best. You were offered everything and had to go and spoil it. It's no good to anyone now. You killed a bird to make it sing. And as for me, who knows, maybe you were my only chance, maybe now I am over-ripe and soon I will start to rot and liquefy like you know who.'

—'Whom,' said Mammy.

—'Over-ripe at twenty?' I asked.

—'Not me?' Mammy asked.

—'And what's so pathetic is it wasn't necessary. It didn't have to fucking happen.'

—'Not me?' Mammy asked again, pointing at her own naked breasts.

—'Yes, you,' said Lucy, 'fucking bloodsucker.'

—'Bloodsucker?'

—'Bloodsucker!'

—'No!'

—'Yes!'

Then Lucy yelped. Mammy had her by the hair and snapped her head back so she was looking at the ceiling whether she liked it or not. Her throat and chin were where her face should be, and her face was on the top of her head, which gave her the air of an adolescent and sensuous Madonna seen from an unflattering angle, as in an Ascension on the ceiling of some damp Venetian palace, to the sound of sloshing waves.

—'Mammy, you're hurting me,' she said in a strained voice.

—'Mammy, stop!' It was Christobel, in from the garden, still hugging her breasts against the cold. 'Let her be,' she said in her blunt, lazy voice, squeezing into the bathroom with us, and she shivered and drew the air through her teeth.

—'Bloody bitch,' said Mammy.

—'Mammy!' said Christobel.

—'Blinking tart,' said Mammy to Christobel, and let go of Lucy to clip Chris's ear. Chris fell down.

Everyone paused to take breath. Even Chris, curled-up half on the bathmat, half off, held her breath.

Lucy, released, was holding the roof of her skull gently in her hands. She staggered slightly and sat down too heavily on the corner of the bath. I could feel the pain she felt as if it were mine, and my eyes were watering. But as I stepped towards Lucy, Mammy caught a handful of my cheek, and twisted it until it ached, and then a dicing pain came through, worse than the worst kind of toothache—the fibres were giving, and my face was coming away from bone like a mask ripped off. She grunted and blew a raspberry with her lips.

—'Let go, Mammy,' I heard Lucy saying, calm and cautious, but in a weakened voice. '*Mammy*!' she shouted. '*Let go!*'

Someone had a hold on my leg. It was Chris, and Lucy kicked her like a football, but she clung on. 'You too Chris, let him go.' Lucy was screaming now, 'You're hurting him.' Tears were running down her face. 'Chris, Mammy, you're hurting him.'

—'What on earth do you think I'm trying to do?' asked Mammy in exasperation, and uttered a few low words in Dutch or German. A feeling of drowning in air—I understood now what Lucy had meant—which made me point down my throat and shake a claw by my head.

Was it that all the negative space in the bathroom *must* be filled—I thought of what students get up to in Minis or telephone boxes, even in beds and in art—whether by a leg, a contortion, a shoe-lace, a grimace. We could use a python in here! But hold the owl!

I thought, too, with that serenity and acceptance which sometimes comes with crisis, of the beautiful Marx bros stateroom skit. But here, meanwhile, it was almost as if the drains had blocked and were back-filling the bathroom with the customary human mass. Like dross I bobbed to the top—an insight on that glaring over-sight of the fifth Marx brother, Karl—and crowd-surfed near the extractor fan with some complacency & technique, until abruptly sucked down again by—one hunts for antique parallels—I suppose it's the *Death of Laocoön's* involutions. But if so—Laocoön having been pythonned merely for distrusting the Trojan horse and its cargo of ruin—well, what was with the horse in our case? Was it concupiscence? Lasciviousnss? Lubricity? Was it just *us?*

Diverse forces, meanwhile, floated me over the bath. My arms, still clawed, had gone behind one leg. I couldn't inhale—in the crush my muscles couldn't move my ribs. Very near my face through a tapestry of winter arms I saw Chris pulling at my foot, twisting it expertly as if to unscrew it as a souvenir, yet frozen in the act of toppling backwards with a face of surprise as I jabbed her with it.

It was a fabric we wove with our limbs and trunks, a rag-like paper, in being stiffly flexible, tight, and 2-D, wrapping itself around each surface that—in its flattened, creaking, bug-like creepering—it came across. Toilet, bath, shower, basin, bidet—all in a tasteful avocado—and even the heated baby-grand towel rail, the bog-brush in the form of an enormous toothbrush (what was *that* trying to tell us?), the chromed toilet roll dispenser. The extractor fan cut in again. And this was when I wondered, dispassionately, are they really going to kill me?

But shedding Christobel had unbalanced us. For a brief instant, as she too fell, I saw sanity flit across Mammy's face. The enamel edge of the bath chopped my skull at a tangent. Lucy, upside down, her face smeared with snot, said 'You've done it now,' in a tearful & exulting voice. My stomach floated upwards like an escaped balloon. Misty patches were roving across my vision like breath, condensing on a mirror, when you want to see what you like like up close, as I lay on top of Chris & Mammy, with Lucy on top of me. It was then we heard, coming from the stairs, the honking of a goose—*Bertie!*

Taking it a step at a time, a little mermaid pointing on agonising joints, he'd come down to see what was up. And realising we were playing a game, he laid his forelegs flat on the ground, his sharp buttocks raised, and barked, switching his tail from side to side, sensuously.

Then, turning his mouth on its side and exposing a set of yellowing fangs, he took my dangling hand gently, and began to tug at it.

He tossed his head about, and danced playfully with his forefeet.

Straining with his back legs, which trembled slightly, he tried to twist the hand off. His teeth, denting my skin like a row of masonry nails, threatened to sink in, as he shook his head about.

Standing up up on his back legs now, he linked forelegs around my arm. He was making vague stamping gestures, and his pelvis was humping and undulating. Christobel, still seated on the floor holding my trainer, was the first to laugh.

—'Bertie, no,' she said. 'Look Mammy, he's masturbating.'

And it was true. Between his legs a little spot of pink protruded from the fur and disappeared, protruded and disappeared.

—'Bertles, no! Not allowed! Sad hound!'

Bertie was panting deep in his chest, and with each pant he made his honking sound. With sudden emotion he drew his coarsened tongue across my cheek, my nose, my open, disbelieving eye.

—'You see he likes the salt,' explained Christobel.

He yawned, releasing my hand with its neat row of perforations, and his jaw dislocated like the jaw of a snake—come to think of it, where *was* the pythoness?—and his eyes squeezed tight. Then his teeth clicked shut and he resumed his hump.

Tears were running down Chris's face, which was frozen in the expression of laughter. She couldn't breathe and couldn't speak. She had irresistible giggles. But Bertie seemed to be addressing us all by means of honks.

He came.

I noticed his eyes were blue.

—'Bertie?' Lucy was asking.

Bertie continued honking. He was opening and closing his mouth like someone savouring something allegedly delicious but in practice disgusting.

He shambled unsteadily back to the foot of the stairs where, like a shallow drift of grey snow, he banked up against the bottom step. A mild squeal, as if someone had pinched him unexpectedly somewhere very tender. And a look of apology, perhaps craven, a submission to the universal malice. Beneath which was a sullen itch to suck what modest joy was still to be had from the blossoms of reality. He closed his eyes and coughed twice. He'd become thinner.

Christobel's laughter, after a long period of silent overload, had again found voice.

—'Don't laugh, Chris, I think Bertie might be dead.'

—'Ooo!,' said their mother, and rose from beneath us, so we all tumbled off and, her fingers twitching at the end of limp forearms, went to see.

—'Rubbish,' said Christobel, 'he's just sleeping. Everyone sleeps after sex, you know that. Answer me, Bertles, are you asleep?'

But Bertie didn't respond. He couldn't see to see.

—'Sweet Bertie, when I was a baby, you were a pup. You've watched over my whole life,' said Lucy.

'Can we bury him in the garden Mammy?' said Christobel.

'Ooo!' said Mammy. 'Do you think he's really dead?'

'O leave him alone,' said Lucy, 'fucking lunatics. Anyway, he was very old. And he had a really good life.'

—'He was very old indeed,' said Christobel solemnly. 'Adorable hound.'

—'Boohoo, boohoo,' said their mother, formally. She lifted her wrist to each eye in turn, but she was smiling.

Christobel, too, sniffed, and then she started crying.

Bertie lay there silently, his woolly body sinking amongst its bones like the ashes of a burnt-out fire.

—'He came to fuck my daughters but instead he killed my dog,' observed Mammy.

—'Can we get a new dog Mammy,' said Christobel.

—'Yes! A puppy for Mammy! It'll lick my face. And stare in my eyes. Like a tiger in the funfair from shooting at metal ducks. So adorable. Please Luce! Pretty please! Or a kitten! Waow! O please!'

Bertie was now no more than the very rug pulled out from under his own four feet.

Lucy kissed me once on the forehead and looked fiercely into my face as if with a slow film in low light she was snapping it.

—'Goodbye now,' she said, accidentally whispering the *now.* 'Gotta go before Mammy cuts up rough.'

—'I thought she already had.'

—'No, she gets violent.'

—'Then I don't want to leave you here,' I said. But Lucy was already pushing me against the stairs until, tripping on Bertie, I fell up them backwards. I so wanted her—not sexually—it was *her,* she was the only thing I ever could want.

—'Just go. Believe me. Before they start saying you killed the dog. It's your last chance. I mean it. Go.'

To my shame, I went.

A light was flickering up there and like an insect I struggled towards it. I found myself crawling about in the hall. The loose tiles rattled in their gums. The walls a shocking pink. I heard Mammy downstairs in her guttural voice instructing the girls.

—'I'm going to *hurt* him. He didn't have to do that. No one asked him to come kill Bertie! Did they?'

And an irresponsible voice saying—

—'You show him, Mammy.'

And a serious voice saying—

—'He didn't Mammy. And he's gone.'

I left the house as giddily as I could, given that I was on all fours. In the front garden it seemed to me the sun was up. Dilute birds were singing, and I stood and stumbled about, having lost myself in a thicket of erect sunflowers with green unshaven legs.

They couldn't help but turn their faces to follow me, forgetting their task was to hide.

I may have slept a bit.

Eventually, between the stalks, I saw them coming. It was a procession—first sombre Christobel, then frowning Mammy wrapped in her breast-nipping towel again, a smaller lilac towel mounded up in her hair. She was tossing her face from side to side in time with her steps, mouthing emphatic refusals. Then came Lucy, smiling privately to herself, carrying slumped Bertikins across her arms like a *Pietá*—his legs, head, tongue, ears, tail all dangling and swinging loosely—towards the dustbin, which was fluted like a peeled muffin and smelt of potato rinds. What is it with these dogs? Is it that they can't help but die?

And what was it with them? Was it that *neither* had wanted me, that they were just trying their strength, the strength of desire that the other shouldn't prevail?

Lucy looked my way, blindly. Mammy stopped for Chris to lift the rubber lid, took Bertie from Lucy's outstretched arms, and then holding him high in one hand, dangling by a hind leg, from an unnecessary height, but with a certain aplomb, she dropped him in face-first with a sullen *DoNgK!*

She made the gesture of cleansing her hands by clashing them sideways like cymbals. Christobel was larking around—the dustbin-lid a coolie hat, and then it became a radar dish. Bleeping laconically, she revolved. Time froze in glacial terror as her cheeping ceased and the dish stalled, wavering in my direction, passed, paused, returned to me again.

But then revolution and cheeping resumed.

Lucy snatched the radar dish from Chris, took a long last look down at Bertie in his galvanised grave, and very softly, so as not to waken him, replaced the rubber lid. Not so much fluted muffin now as hollow column, a broken one.

Then they all went in through the red front door and slammed it behind them, making the door-knocker knock. The knocker a prancing horse in dulled brass, its tail up but kinked. Was it just Bertie's ghost, wanting back in?

Someone turned the telly up full, and there were bursts of canned laughter and bursts of real—cascades of light-headed giggles—as if their skulls could hinge open and joy come out. I heard water sploshing. And then, above the telly and the water, *Stille Nacht*, sung in two-part harmony, for some reason in German. Lucy and Christobel both sang alto, in unison, but at an interval of a fifth, whilst Mammy, a carrying and a competent treble, wove tangled and even flailing under-harmonies around their steady, lovable voices, conveying, though it was already daylight, far deeper mysteries than mere annunciation and nativity.

Cutting across the common, I wandered home limping, not because my ankle hurt, but because I'd cast a shoe.

Would Luce try the feet with it of countless men?

Girlie

> When I do count the clock that tells the time,
> And see the brave day sunk in hideous night.
> (Shakespeare, *Sonnet XII.)*

One of his eyes was always a little bloodshot, and his skin was clear and pale with tints of black and green beneath it. He had that look of distrustful cunning worn by profound but simple people who have been done once too often, and are always looking for the catch in innocent proposals. His trash-blond hair was so fine and straight that it looked like it would give you paper-cuts and made you want to keep your hands away. It came down in jagged points over his ears and over the collar of his woolly shirt. He wore his top shirt-button closed. A red check lumber-jacket gave a deceptive neatness to his appearance. His tucked-in nose and dished, little-boy face made strangers cluster round him in pubs.

—'I'm under the *affluence* of *incohol,*' he told me, and I could smell the slight sick on his breath.

Above us, the sun wheeled behind a steeple black and trembling with ivy. When the wind blew, it went pale in sliding patches.

Then, dogged, ponderous, in hum, tierce and quint, a clock struck six on the tower's bell.

—'Eleven;' he said soberly, his dished face quite straight, 'nine; five; eight; two; ...' and every leaf on the tower shuddered like flesh in the wind with his culminating: 'Six!'

Then he instantly cracked his irresistible smile.

Was there a secret behind his jumbled numbers? This I asked, and he didn't answer that question, but another.

Beneath our feet we could feel the vibration of a tube train passing, and it seemed to me, though I knew it couldn't be, that *this* had rung the bell.

—'What'll it be?' he asked gamely, before fading into the dark intestine of the pub with a significant face, coming back with foaming glasses.

The underside of his chin pulsed as he sucked at his golden drink, his head tilted back, eyes closed, and the corners of his mouth drawn down.

—'Like fucking spring water,' he said and sighed, fluttering blonde lashes attractively. A beautiful man, but his plump lips, if you looked close, were stiffened with a mild spite, and his clothes and hair smelt of smoke.

—'I tell a lie,' he added with a shiver, holding up the half-empty glass for me to see before he took another swig. 'Cool as the period of a nun!'

He could be vulgar, coarse, out-of-order. Made a point of it, even, to frame his ethereal face. Much later we went on to a discotheque.

We knew it was a discotheque because music was thudding like the tube, underneath the pavement. And the grid of pavement lights, set flush in burred and sanded asphalt, kept time in a hypnotic cycle of purple, green and pink.

—'Hullo Wilk' said the bouncer in an impossibly deep voice which emerged from a beard itself greyish, red. He wore a look of weary innocence, like a man watching a riot in the distance.

—'Hello,' said Wilk vaguely, smiling suddenly with his teeth.

Downstairs, the club had the fire-blackened ceiling and undulating walls of a cave. Hot girls, tired of dancing, sat about on sticky leatherette, waiting for something or other. Wilk had already found a clearing on the raised dance-floor and, pulsing purple and lurid, flung his hands up, manacled; looked sharply over either shoulder, eyes shut; and then slowly bent his legs, knees glued—to twist. It was his signature dance, familiar as the stars.

A girl danced past him, seemed to linger, and danced away. She had a restless trotting dance, her thighs chafing through scuffed and glossy black-leather trousers, her behind describing sudden angular curves. Her rib-cage jiggled to a different beat whilst her head hung still and glum above this corporal mess. Crouching near the ground now, in comical slo-mo, Wilk danced backwards after her.

Eventually, in a pre-established harmony, they came to face each other in the centre of the floor, she and Wilk, turning all kinds of unexpected colours under the showers of light. She was holding in her outstretched hand a burning fag, and every so often, without opening her eyes, she raised it to her lips. Wilk's eyes, too, stayed shut.

But every so often one or other would do a tribal jog gravely round on the spot, wagging a loose finger at the sky. And Wilk—he was warming up. Now a turkey was hastening round the dance-floor, now a lamb was gambolling on a flooded lawn. And now a cat pounced on mice, but each time it lifted its furry claws—no mouse! And finally, with a flourish and a flap, a cockerel asserted his just dominion over the heaving, strobing, deafening stack-yard of dance.

When the music ended they smiled humourlessly and left the floor. Wilk's face when he came up was sticky and there were small clusters of spittle in the corners of his lips. Looking down, be made himself a double-chin as he carefully undid the top button of his woolly shirt. Then he took up the beer-bottle I'd brought him, with its cringe-inducing tagline—*Proud to be the Bottle of Britain*—and showed me his teeth.

—'I'd rather a full bottle in front of me than a full frontal lobotomy,' he announced.

And he then emitted his beautiful fixed grin which, charming & wary, for some reason always made me think of Red Riding Hood's cape. It shone like a moral lamp, blinding, not because his teeth were glaring in that plastic Hollywood way—but because his pukka face and jagged, white-blond hair were bright and alluring, reminiscent of Goldmund or Little Lord Fauntleroy, though he lacked their depth.

The DJ, wearing shades and a ten-gallon hat, spun an LP on his finger before letting it sink onto the turntable. A monstrous, plaintive rapper began. Wilk's partner was already out on the floor, trotting pert on the spot in time to the patter, drawing sensuously on her fag. Her leather trousers had stretched into sagging purses at the knees and in the buttocks. Her naked belly sank inwards above her hips, as if she were sucking it in, and she wore a stiff leather tank-top resting on her breasts and exposing their undersides, and slashed with undone zips through which you saw flashes of skin. Taking up his *Bottle of Britain,* Wilk hipped urgently towards her and, by way of a pairing ritual, she swigged at it as he drew upon her fag. Dance once over, he brought her back to present to me.

She advanced with her legs together, as if she were clenching her buttocks.

—'Meet Girlie.'
—'Hello Girlie.'
—'Hello,' she said through her smile, hardly moving her lips. Please to meet you,' she added.
—'Hello Girlie' said Wilk in a low droll voice.
—'Hello,' she said again, smiling pointedly. 'I'm a post-feminist,' she told us quickly.
—'Really?' I said.
—'Post-feminist?' asked Wilk.
—'Yes.'
—'Meaning?'
—'Meaning I don't hate men.'

It was a joke. Her brown, vague irises were concealed under her upper eyelids, and she had a dull ring embossed in her skin under each eye. Dark, lightless, very sad, her eyes seemed to run like mascara down her face.

Her skin was the colour of full-cream milk and her nose, mouth and eyes were delicately cut. There was a ripe pimple, on the point of bursting, off-centre to her chin. Her hair was dyed a matt blue-black, *farouched* with too much gel. She presented as the subsidiary love-interest in a horror film, caught in a downpour on the way to the set.

His eyes, on the other hand—a mineral blue whose ink was leaching into his whites; and a self-effacing, cheeky, yet smug smile beneath that pretty, *retroussé* nose. In clothing, he leant towards duck or twill in mushroom, taupe, beige—worn with a red check lumber-jacket and a reversed baseball cap.

—'Ah, you'll want to hear my disabled jokes then,' he said, eager to outclass her in tastelessness. Luckily, he forgot to tell us them.

When at last the lights came up and everyone was gone, they started sweeping out the place and we bought two half-pints of vodka at a rip-off price. Girlie asked us back.

She lived on the same block as the club, and I remember the stok-stok-stok of her zipped and affecting black-leather orthopaedic boots, of the sort child polio-survivors used to wear, over the gritty pavements, together with the faint sound of dripping rain. Slung between *punk* and *goth*, she erred on the side of punk. *And* goth.

She fished for her latchkey in her knickers, and as she opened the door with a suggestive, thrilling giggle, a wet cat streaked in off the street and up into the dark. We clustered together in the small hallway, because there was stuff she needed to explain to us.

—'That's *my* cat,' she boasted. 'Well, to tell you the honest truth, my lover really! True story.' And she giggled.
—'Yes?'
—'Yes. I call him *Shit.* My other one was *Pissy.* Pissy was having kittens that I give him more piercings so he run away. He was a only a little kitten, see, and he come wrapped-up in Chrissy paper with a bow and a holly, a prezzie from my ex. But because of his ferrety fur *and* pink eyes!, I call him Pissy. They go together, see?'

—'*I tort I saw a pissy cat, a-creeping up on me,*' Wilk sang, and to the extent possible in this cramped hallway, he dangled his hands at the end of extended forearms, raising successive knees to his chin to creep up on Girlie.
—'Hehe,' she said. 'Eek! But anyways now he's called Clitty instead because it's a better name because it rhymes and in case he come back to me for some more piercings, see.'

I could see she'd caught Wilk's entire attention, something not easy to do.

—'You don't say!' he said, eventually.

—'Here Shitty-Shitty,' she was calling up into the darkness, and Shit reappeared magically at her feet, performing sinuous figures-of-eight between her legs. He stared up at her, and opening his mouth, after a pregnant pause he mewed through fish-white teeth.

—'What? ... the devil!' said Wilk.

—'Here Clitty-Clitty,' she added hopefully. Shit ceased his weaving and sat there a few steps up, erect, proud, indifferent, his face turned away not only from Girlie but from each of us. His tail, laid like a pretty muff over his paws betraying, in a faint but angry flicker of its blunt tip, a patient irritation. We waited hopefully, but Clit never came. 'I'm telling you, see,' she said, 'Clit run away on me. He dumped me. They all do, in the end.

To tell you the honest truth, I don't care. There's always a better cat, is how I sees it.'

It was time to go in. As we felt our way up the turning staircase in the dark, all I could see was the faintest image, like a negative, of Wilk's hands spread, melodramatically, one on each of Girlie's leather buttocks.

And also Shitty's smug absence from visibility, his lithe black form—he didn't care who knew it—being merely a cut-out from a phenomenal reality, disclosing what was underneath.

With the grate of an egg-shell breaking, she turned a mortise-key, also from her knickers, in the lock. The smell which came out of her flat then was of rancid butter and overheated dust.

—'Come, come,' she said, closing the door behind us. And just like Shit, the hinges mewed.

An orange streetlamp outside her window turned us all old.

Girlie lit an enormous candle in the shape of a mauve phallus with her *Bic* lighter, and with the same flame and trembling fingers, tilted her head to light a further fag.

Hanging on the blackboard-paint wall she had a blow-up skeleton, with buck-teeth, playing a guitar. The guitar had an arrowhead soundbox irresistibly reminiscent of a *Ford Anglia* with its reverse-rake rear window, suggestive in turn of a cheese-slice. Glowing with some kind of ultraviolet effect, he had a real yellow bandana tied around his forehead, the ends dangling over his left shoulder like a hank of hair.

—'Dude Skellington's like me,' she said. He's a goth.'

She punched him, which made him star-jump whilst strumming violently, and his plastic hide made a raspberry squeak.

—'*What would the duke of Wellington—Make of the music of Duke Ellington?*' I asked.
—'Mad, bad Byron!' Wilk said knowledgeably.
—'Dude Skell's my mate, ain't you Skell. You'n Shitty.'

Looking up at each of us in turn, Shitty mewed, self-consciously *cantabile*.

—'Yeah-yeah Shitty! You's the best!'

We heard the unlocalised rumble of a bass purr, which turned out not to be Shitty at all, but the first tube-train of the day, enlivening the clay beneath our feet.

—'Yeah Shitty, yeah, you's the one to stick by Girlie. Yeah.'

Wilk broke the paper seal on the lid of one of the vodkas. Tossing away the cap and fitting the bottle to his lips, whilst bending his knees too far and raising his face, he lifted it like a bugle to blare at successive quarters of a low sky, one hand brushing the floor behind him as he turned. Girlie, meanwhile, gave Shitty his dinner, letting him eat it straight from the tin.

—'That's how he likes it,' she says. 'Shitty doesn't like to wait.'

Apart from Dude Skellington up on his wall, there was only a bare ticking mattress under a single window, and a black-vinyl easy-chair, where I sat.

—'The mattress, the mattress!' Wilk said. He was laughing so he couldn't finish. 'It's ticking like a clock,' he managed, eventually.
—'Ticking like a bomb more like,' I said.
—'Boom-boom!' said Girlie, diffuse and automatic.

She had opened the front door of her bedsit again. She *tokked* out into the stairwell on her orthopaedic heels, the chrome buckles on her leather jacket jangling dully with the sound of wet coins. Her toilet was a cupboard on the landing, and leaving the cupboard door open she squatted in shadows. Then, chuckling with inviting happiness she came strutting back into the room, pulling her trousers only half up and swirling around like a dancer on tiny wobbling steps so her legs never came apart.

—'I just *love* being nude,' she said. 'Don't you just love it, boys?'

—'Brava, brava!' replied Wilk and clapped his hands and, flinging his white-blonde feathery fringe around, stamped his feet in a *jaleo*, raising dust from the floor. Then he sank back on the mattress, resting on his arms, to watch.

There was no contour to Girlie's buttocks, which sagged behind her, by the light of the sodium street-lamp and the burning mauve phallus, in a kneaded lump. Seemingly moulded from the very pale clay through which the tubes beneath our feet were passing, it was mottled with bruises, with a coarse finger-line scored down the centre and, as she bent invitingly to pet Shit, a deep finger-hole poked in.

And a weal of bright spots on either side of the crack.

Leather trousers still hanging around her knees, she plumped down next to Wilk on the naked mattress and shifted about to settle herself. Then she took away his bottle.

—'Oy!' says Wilk, peevishly.

—'No-No-No,' she said firmly, tick-ticking her finger in time in his face. 'Seriously, Wilk my love, you've already had enough. It'll stop you getting it up. Hehe! Eek!'

She threw back her head to swig.

When she'd had enough herself, she drew her wrist across her mouth and passed the bottle back to him.

—'On second thoughts, go for it,' she said.

Wilk was looking suddenly apprehensive.

—'Will the tubes be running yet?' he asked tentatively.
—'Yes' I said, covering his escape, 'I heard it.'

But Girlie lifted her hand towards his face.

—'Shush...' she told him, pushing her finger slowly between his lips. Struggling more feebly now, like a waterlogged spider, he tried once more.

—'*Let's go,*' he said.

Girlie frowned and withdrew her finger. She stood up with decision but difficulty, her trousers slipping towards her knees, and waddled to me.

—'Here, you,' she said sweetly, bending over me and incidentally showing Wilk her spreading behind. 'Yeah you. *You've* got a sweet smile, *you* just give me a smacker if he wants to be uptight. Just a little smacker, yeah?'

Wilk was grumbling in the background. 'Bend down and crack a smile,' he said pugnaciously. 'Bend down and *crack* a smile. Hah!'

She opened her knees as far as the trousers would let her.

—'You're not a virgin, I can see that,' he called out, helpful, from behind.

—'She's not a virgin,' he was saying, more thoughtfully now, to himself. And as Girlie pressed her open mouth against mine, so that I could feel her teeth on my lips, she unexpectedly took my hand and forced it flat against the stiff lips of a burning, slobbery crotch.

—'Oy,' said Wilk, angry on his mattress. 'Steady on you two.'

Slow off the mark, I turned my face aside and pulled my hand back.

—'Fuck it,' Wilk was saying as he tossed about his head in feathery waves. 'Leave off Girlie, you're out of order, come on, leave off right now. Fuck that!'

Mission accomplished, Girlie waddled back and, when I judged she wasn't looking, I scraped my greasy palm on the vinyl armrest.

—'Here, Shitty-Shitty,' I said—lateral thinking being a speciality. Shitty came to me and mewed, dabbing at the fabric of my trousers with his needle-coloured claws while I gave him a thorough stroking.

Wilk had a fixed smile as Girlie returned, pausing to cross her arms and lift the leather tank-top over her head. The zip-pulls tingled and her soft breasts came out.

—'Come, Girlie,' he said again with authority, and he gave me a finger-up sign. 'You can fucking piss off. Yes, you with the hair on!'

But Girlie plocked here and there across the dirty floorboards, trying to work her leathers over the orthopaedic stiletto boots. She plumped beside Wilk and whimpered as he got the boots off for her, and then the leathers. Under the leathers she was what they call commando-style, naked, but for flamboyant inks and piercings. As Will lay back on the mattress, she wriggled hissing up him, doing her plump yet bony snake-bit. Unlike her buckles, which had jangled, it would be truer to say her piercings jingled.

The mauve phallus spittered and a white smoke-ring slid up, dispersing slowly between us like a contrail.

—'Fock,' said Girlie.
—'... this for a lark!' Wilk capped.

And Girlie giggled and he sighed.

Through the window, the sky was going violet and a single bird sang out loud. In the street beneath, inviting as asylum, a taxi trundled by, yearning for a fare. Girlie was whispering something more in Wilk's ear. They both giggled, sat up to suck vodka, lay down to whisper again.

—'Fock,' whispered Girlie.
—'... this for a lark,' capped Wilk.

But it was no longer her ear he was whispering into, but her lips, and her shivering hand came up the back of his neck and screwed his face onto hers. They rolled sideways on the mattress, wrestled and groaned, lay still.

—'I'm sore for you, Wilk' whispered Girlie, and she caressed her grisly pubic hair with a winning smile.
—'Don't get sore get evil,' capped Wilk.

The virtue of his puns, sometimes suggestive, always out of focus, was that using discomfort they enabled him, like metre or teaching, to point to where there *might* lie truth.

He began breathing-in deeply, perhaps to intoxicate himself on air, just as a would-be amputee gets drunk on cognac before the operation.

—'What?' asked Girlie.
—'... the devil!' Wilk capped.

To tell the honest truth, he couldn't help it. Most of us can't but be ourselves.

I heard them whispering again, and giggling, and more silence. Girlie made a gentle sound at the bottom of her register, a *hauwa*. The pale shape of Wilk's hand was strumming her naked crotch and her loose thighs swung wide. I could see his eyes and teeth reflecting sodium orange. Dark, the shape of his tongue flicked across his teeth.

—'*Hauwa*,' she said again, very low and hardly voiced.

—'Wilk, time to go!' I heard myself say unexpectedly in a dissonant and cheerful key. 'We'll catch the tube.'

But it was much too late.

—'Fucking Piss Off.'

He said the words one by one, slowly, and awkwardly. Reaching up behind the fluffy blond back of his head, which had Girlie's fingers outspread in it, he showed me the front of his middle-finger again.

—'Hehe!' said Girlie, and she giggled, and he giggled back.

—'Fucking Piss Off!' he said again, but his words were stifled by her nibbling lips.

More whispering, the purring of a zip, and a slow, plaintive 'Ohh' from Girlie, and a 'Shit!' from him which caused Shitty to raise his head briefly, before she started undulating, as if drifting on lapping ripples a few inches above his chest. His hands came groping blindly down her back, and gripping and spreading the cheeks of her bottom exposed the rose of her arsehole which, lit by sodium street-lamp, mouthed and flared in slow-time.

Eventually she pushed herself up on her arms, arching her back, and then blowing, as if to cool *Ovaltine,* she panted once, sharply, having scorched her tongue, and then she said *Orner,* and sank a little, and a blanket of piss, *pétillante* and warm spread gently over Wilk's hips, running down the creases on either side of his crotch. Wilk had lifted his head to ask 'What... the devil?' and now he dropped it back, his eyes shut, and I could see from his throat that he swallowed twice.

Girlie backfired like a motorbike, farting a single sharp fart. The pungent, viscous smell of her gut snaked up my nostrils and, when I could no longer hold my breath, slithered down my windpipe to my lungs. Observing this as if it were happening to someone else, someplace else, I couldn't get *indole* out of my mind. Except in the end by embracing an immersive sense—through scent and resonance—of transitting the secret chamber, tangled admittedly, knotted and loose, but otherwise shaped in the form of a snake coiling out its journey to the precise but moving part of the universe it needed to reach—her mouth. *Sometimes the best way out is through,* says Frost.

After some moaning and some cries they both went slack. Their hoarse panting slowed to gentleness. Eventually they slept. Huddled in the vinyl easy-chair, in the blue-eyed dawn, Shit on my lap, we slept too.

When I woke the window was a blinding oblong, like the light above an operating table. A succulent bluebottle was whirring and bumping on the glass and the room stank of breathlessness, sex, heat. A carton of off-milk had capsized in the night and a gruelly mound of curds had formed round the spout. Wilk and Girlie had rolled apart—Wilk and Shit were now curled up together, while Girlie was lying diagonally on her back, her top half off the mattress, with her arms and her legs apart and her breasts hanging up. Daylight disclosed naked floorboards littered with crumpled knickers, old *McDonald's* cartons, and a scatter of empty miniatures. The ticking mattress between the sleeping bodies was studded with kidney shaped stains of spunk, and rust-tinted stains of blood. And on one wall, imperfectly obscured by Dude Skellington's skinny legs, there was a swung arc of shiny, ancient, spattered blood.

Girlie sniffed in her sleep, and scratched in the hairs of her crotch. She lifted her head suddenly, scrunching her eyes against the light. Then she propped herself on her elbow to light a fag, drew manically, and dammed her *farouche* black hair back out of her eyes. Her legs were so thin that her knees became knotty lumps in a rope. Just like Dude's.

When she stood she wobbled, a foal standing for the first time. Her skin was scarred with the rucks in the mattress and the gaps in the floorboards, her arms were spattered with moles, and on her belly you could see lumps like raisins under the transparent skin. A pimple had burst in the night, and weeped minutely onto her chin. Walking lightly on bare feet, she made it out to the toilet and sat down heavily there, making various flamboyant sound effects.

Shit yawned next, showing a curling tongue of perfect lilac set amongst fish-bone teeth. His claws came out and then went in again. Clocking the toppled milk he hurried silently across, stiff tail high and swaying. He chewed the curds in the side of his mouth with a jabbing movement of his head.

And Wilk was sitting up now. His hair was mussed like the grass at a picnic, and he seemed concussed. He scrabbled his fingers over his blond fluffy scalp, blinked, and looked about himself in surprise. Observing that he was naked he spread a hand shaped like an enormous leaf over his crotch whilst making a defensive face, as if he detected that, just as he'd feared, yet again he'd been done. But through it a yawn erupted, puckering his lips off his yellow teeth and clenching up his pin-prick eyes, his elegant features half crumpled, half stretched in delight.

—'Quick, before she comes back, what's her name?' he whispered quickly.
—'Girlie.'
—'I can hear everything!' she said severely from her station on the landing.

—'We're just nipping out for a drink, Girlie,' he said. 'Nipping out for a nip!' he capped, in a voice which came out too loud.

—'Hehe,' she said, aggressively.

Then he fed each leg into his trousers with the burning concentration of someone pouring hot liquid down a blocked pipe. Girlie, visible through the open door still seated majestic in the toilet cupboard, her hands gripped between her thighs, was yawning herself.

—'See you later?' asked Wilk.

—'Who do ya think you're kidding?' Girlie asked, and yawned again. 'The vodka stays here—what's left of it. Don't be getting clever.'
—'I wouldn't dream of it,' said Wilk.

—'You too, the peeping voyeur or what have you?' she said to me. 'I could get you both done.'

There was white-out in the street. The pavement was white and the road was a bright, bright grey. Wilk's face had no definition, reduced to small black eyes and dusted hair on a powdery, flawless complexion—was it—a clock face! As we walked he was knocking at his skull with the heel of his palm as if it was an old-fashioned television which had lost its vertical hold.

—'Whatever happened?' he asked me after an interval, in the tone of a bystander at an accident.
—'Afraid you screwed,' I said.
—'... up!' he capped. 'But no, impossible!'

The pub was just re-opening, and Wilk, looking dubious, sank into the dull interior to buy the first drinks. The floor was clearly flat, but he seemed to be going downhill. I could hear him clearly, counting out his change, with a fascination he was not afraid to voice, onto the bar.

—'What's with the random numbers, I don't understand?' I asked when he came back out.
—'Random? You so sure? Maybe there's no such thing in the multiverse. Anyways, if there's one thing *I* don't understand—it's how could you have let me? With her I mean,' he asked in disbelief, slowing down for emphasis on the last few words. 'She was repulsive. *Fucking* repulsive. How could you?'
—'How could you?' I answered unhelpfully. 'Because I didn't. You did.'

But he was sulking and didn't answer me.

—'Don't mind if I do,' he hinted later, and I went in to refill the drinks.

—'The thing about drinking, you know what it is? It just makes you thirsty' he said, and took a swig. 'Ah, *Chin-chin, Salut, Skål,*' he added with traditional saloon-bar courtliness. 'Here's mud in your eye!' he said with zest.

Above us, the clock on its trembling tower began to strike and his face shone with delight.

—'Nineteen,' said Wilk, 'five, forty-seven, six, three, minus one, eleven, five no I've had five, six argh!, orange, green, virtue, faith ...'

And then he paused, waiting, his mouth open, and ducking his dished and handsome face with complacent finality shouted: *'Twelve!'* And before he took a further swig, he whooped quietly if joyously, jerking his head about with a fixed smile as he looked up at the racing clouds and the sun, behind the ivy-mangled tower and the clock.

—'Twelve noon,' he said, 'well fancy that!'

When the wind blew, the ivy went white.

—'Doth put lead in your pencil, lager.'
—'And ink in your pen.'
—'And pus in your boil, it doth.'
—'Please Wilk, less graphic, on top of last night.'
—'Still,' he said, exhaling slowly before he went in for refills, tapping my

shoulder before continuing in an offensive Indian take-away voice: *I'd rather a full bottle in front of me than a full frontal lobotomy.'*

And he took-in a deep breath which tightened the woolly shirt, its top button done up neatly, across his breast.

—'Wouldn't you? Wouldn't anyone?' he asked, huffing his breath out suddenly so his shoulders sagged.
—'Well ...'

But he was looking angry again. He'd remembered Girlie.

—'How could you let me? How could you fucking let me? You hairy arse-hole.' He was laughing in wonder and disgust. But his hands were making as if to claw out his eyes. He looked apprehensively at each hand in turn as they approached.

—'What was I *thinking!* he said.
—'You weren't.'

His penis had compromised his face.

Clutching at handfuls of sharp, white-blonde hair he threw his head back, went down on one knee and bared his teeth.

—'Aaargh!' he shouted. 'Arreggh! Ai-ai-ai! Bother!'

And then, walking back and forth on on both knees in the gutter, he held his lowered face in his hands for a time, his elbows pressed into his sides, like someone counting to one hundred in *it.*

I saw the vertical wrinkles in front of his ears, as if he'd pulled his face on too tight.

—'She gives you the willies,' he said, suddenly looking up like a child and showed me his winning teeth. 'Talk about goth, but she *punks* goth. Punks goth!' he said, capping himself. 'Or is it that she goths punk?' he wondered.

—'Couldn't you see I was absolutely blotto! Talk about drunkard's remorse! Ouch! The kind of feeling which you can't tell if it was the drink which feels it or you for what you done. I mean—you know what I mean. And it's not good enough to say it's the alcohol what did it, not you—I mean—what if she's preggers! Alcopop or not, imagine it!'

Then he sank into darkness with our empty glasses for refills.

—'Hair of the dog,' he commented. 'Down the hatch,' he said. And he grimaced and lapped at the golden stuff.

—'I'm remembering!,' he said.

He was examining the pavement, but his blue eyes, one bloodshot and one clear, came suddenly up to mine.

—'Did you see her piss on me?'
—'I smelt it, too.'
—'Sex is a funny thing.'
—'Isn't it?'
—'There's no accounting for taste.'
—'You don't say!'
—'TSSssss,' he said, 'ffrrartrip...POP!,' and he laughed so much that his fine face went red and tears fell out of his eyes.

Suddenly he gave at the knees as if someone had punched him in the stomach. He was struggling to speak.

—'What?' I asked him, 'What?'
—'Parson's,' he squeaked eventually.
—'What?'
—'Parson's ...' he tried in another register. Tears were running on his face.
—'Yes?'
—'Parson's *nose*,' he said and gulped, and then his voice went high, 'with *lashings* of gravy.' And very low again, to a super-slow beat, 'Yum! Yum! Yum!'

But he was interrupted by his own coughing and, pressing his palm flat against his ribcage to calm his clamorous lungs, with the other hand he fished about in his jacket pocket, searching for his cigarettes. He lit-up and squinting at me, drew.

—'She was revolting,' he said, allowing twin streams of smoke to flow from his nostrils.

—'Not as nice as she looked,' I said. Only by daylight, as, bewildered, we had all been moving round her room, had I noticed she had tiny numbers inked around the rim of a face which otherwise resembled, in its deathly pallor and barring the zits, those not-yet painted carnival masks you can buy in art shops to hint at a personal gaiety.

Wilk had paused to work it out.

—'Now that's not fair. Don't knock Girlie. It's just not true. You cunt!'
—'Cool it,' I said. 'Then what about plain, but nice,' by way of mending fences.
—'Cunt,' he said again. 'She wasn't plain, she was darned ugly.'
—'Nobody is ugly. We are all miracles. Miraculous, but nice.'
—'Nice?'
—'She looked like death!'
—'...warmed up,' he capped.

Yet he still scowled, nettled.

—'Yes,' I said.
—'Fucking necrophilia.'
—'Yes.'

At last his gloomy face brightened.

—'You know, I used to *be* a necrophiliac,' he told me. He was never gloomy for long.
—'Yes?'
—'Till some rotten cunt split on me.'

—'Ouch.'
—'Mind you, I probably didn't smell so sweet either come to think of it. Last night I mean.'
—'Nope.'
—'Corpse fucks corpse.'
—'Corpses fuck.'

The earth beneath our feet rumbled as a train, presumably brightly lit and packed with genuine people, passed.

And now we stood there still, outside the pub, like an old couple who no longer needed to speak. Eventually the clock struck.

—'One,' said Wilk quietly, once. 'That girl's an accident waiting to happen.'
—'Girlie?'
—'She's a solution looking for a problem.'
—'Really?'

—'All dressed up and nowhere to go!'
—'She was naked last time I saw her.'
—'Shut your face.'

Above us, emitting its foul noises, ferrying the cowed, an airliner passed.

—'She's okay,' he said, reflectively, and he rinsed some beer between his lips and his teeth.
—'Who, Girlie?'
—'Girl's alright.' He sounded nostalgic and almost weepy. 'Just try to tell me she ain't,' he threatened.
—'No, no,' I said.
—'She's gotta lotta bottle,' he said.
—'Lotta bottle,' I said.
—'She rattled those fanny rings like a tambourine!
—'Or even a castanet!'

Another plane came over. What was it with those planes?

It was like the *Bottle of Britain*, only worse.

—'You know, I'm feeling I'd like to say my respectful goodbyes property. No, prop-op-op-operly! After all, we did fu-fu-fuck.'
—'Up.'

We drank in silence.

—'So I'm going back,' he announced suddenly, in the over-deep tones of a theatrical knight. 'I may be a little time,' he said, handing me his empty glass.
—'You sure about that goodbye? Not *hello-hello-hello, what have we here, gorgeous?'*

He turned his face suddenly to mine, hurt and a little angry, and held my gaze and held his breath. The shape of his mouth expressed a bewildered discomfort, like a man discovering mutiny amongst his limbs. As usual, he was seeking the catch.

—'Well, maybe,' he said eventually, letting it out, and he darted me a suspicious look. 'Besides, I hope there's some vodka left.'

I dropped the empty glasses inside the pub, and we walked together to her doorway, where Wilk took my hand.

—'Bye,' he said to me with feeling.
—'Bye Wilk'.
—'We had ourselves a ball. Two, even. Though not, this time, four. Sorry about that.'
—'No problem!' I said quickly.

His eyes, one reddened, were glistening.

—'Drank too much.'
—'Yes.'
—'We always do. Bye then. Look after yourself.'
—'Yes, bye. Take care, Wilk.'

I haven't seen him since.

But as I walked away I looked up and saw she'd printed the word

LECHERY

in white spooky letters across her window, probably in curdled milk.

Can of Dreams

I am a graveyard that the moon abhors.
(Baudelaire.)

—The floorboards were hidden by swelling banks of nettles and clumps of wispy thistles. So the bedroom had this spiked mundane smell of nettles, and the heavenly smell of thistles. There were too many stags in her dressing room to move around freely. Their flanks were smoking, and you could see their breath and smell fell hide. And, if you looked close, see vermin on the move through their pelts, which made her think of women labouring through a thicket, tearing their auburn hair on brambles & thorns. And, and the antlers made the click of knitting or typing when they touched, however gently. Or else the clack of pool.
—Mad, I said.

As we walked, she drew back her face and observed me through a rent veil of hair, which trembled.

—Between their legs scuttled badgers, and stoats between theirs, and then voles, she said.
—Nested quadrupeds.
—Beneath the floor delved moles, throwing up splintered wood. The bedroom ceiling was invisible behind a curtain of wisteria, honey-suckle and the lower leaves of an enormous lime. You could hear bees.
—All this signified the remote future of her room—the traveller, in her lab, fitting the ebon and ivory rods, mounts a pulsing machine. Or else its past?
—Only, in the kitchenette, a colt-pony as she called him was at the fridge, lifting neat hairy knees and stomping on the frosted shelves. He was guzzling on lettuce, cellophane, and marmalade from a shivered jar, his nose matted with marmalade and blood.
—Oh.

In the grass around us, which was a saturated autumn green over a matte-yellow lower growth, were set rakish monuments in pristine granite, weathered slate, effaced sandstone, dissolute limestone. They bobbed subliminally as we passed, as if the whole place was set on a trampoline.

—We build our homes of brick and tin but our graves of stone, I said.
—And our bodies of meat and skin.
—The graves must last longest.

—Go on.
—Meantime, back on the bed, her dog, Sherry or *Chérie*, I never knew which, and there was no which, maybe, since she was both honey-colour and loved, lay between her slightly parted legs. With her ears limp and a shamed glow in her eyes, which wouldn't meet the shamed glow in mine. Her muzzle, as my Nan spoke, rested on Nan's balding mount of Venus, risible under a lawn nighty trimmed with lace daisies and lace marigolds.
—I see.

Around us as she spoke, tormented and chilled beneath the quilted grass, lay spines and skulls and jaws set in jellied beds of human mush.

—Look! Look! said my Nan, in utter joy. A beige fawn leaps out through the casement, and prances in the herbaceous borders and bounds the picket fence with its twisted rails! Now it's wolfing gloxinias and liriodendron leaves which it gathers into its mouth with a shiny maroon tongue, coarse and plump. Greedy devil! But something is wrong with all the flowers! They look like piles of bones! She was delirious, you see, she said.
—Yes.

Now—

Deadly Beloved,
Live as if you are dying,
Because you are

advised a mirror-finish monument which, walking in step, we passed. Speckled as a grey egg, it was a favourite roost, and was adorned with the lime of bird-shit tainted with the mauve of blackberries.

—I'd like something like that, I said, when my time comes!
—When your time comes? It's too late. *This* is your time. It's come.
—You know what I mean.
—And almost gone.

Many of the graves, in the spirit in which people wrap up their car-seats, sofas, food and flowers, were wrapped in cling film, cinched round the base with ribbon, gaffer tape, twine. Even a mite, asleep in a nearby pushchair whilst its parent tinkered with the scented candles and soft toys of a small, fresh grave, was wrapped in cellophane like the flowers, and had cheeks of edible wax, flushed with a little food-colouring.

—And, and there is a rook with blue feathers and a white choker perched on my lampshade, she told me, she said, his shellac, scaled claws denting lemon watered-silk. Listen, it may interest you to hear, dear bird, she told the rook, that I was once shy! *Caw!* was its reply.

Her face, through the rents in her hair, trembled.

—And, my dear bird, she went on severely, Christ is come. *Caw! Caw!* Shush! *Caw!* Shush! *Caw!* But if He goes deeper than me, believe me I have had the more interesting life.
—Than Christ?
—Yes, Christ! Then she wiped the back of her hand across her slack mouth and blinked her eyes. Can you see Him? I asked her softly. Of course not! she said, cross. Sometimes, pet, you're insufferably dim. Christ was, she then confided in a rising voice, as if about to sneeze or come, a Quisling, a cat's paw, yes a puppet of God's! Yes? I asked. *Yea!*, she said, emphatic. His stigmata were bored for strings.
—No strings attached! I said. This semi-crass remark my friend ignored.

—Being paralysed I wish to embark first, she then said, in a crystalline enunciation like someone at the dawn of radio. Please indicate what time I shall be carried on board. Her eyes became lovely, & she held out her arms to divine Charon, dark against the open casement, & grinned.

Her hand, my friend's, as she walked and told me this, lay sweaty in my hand. It was also supernaturally articulate, even voluble. It hinted that I too was loved, or might be.

—She then made a gargling sound with her throat, as naturally as if it were a continuation of conversation by other means, she said. I got into bed beside her. I closed her eyes. Closed mine, which were on fire and floating in tears which felt not clear but violet, as if the colour inside my eyes had run. When in the end she went I felt like she had just been born someplace else, as in *when you dream, another awakes.* Leaving me home alone. My nose was running, so I used her sheet.

I imagined a glass paperweight, globular as a snow-dome and floored in fluted glass flowers, set in a dingy windswept room; fluttering nets, the sun reflected in a puddle outside making shimmers across the ceiling, and my friend drying her cheeks on her grandmother's shroud.

—Then Chérie started barking at someone I couldn't see, not in excitement, with a wagging tail, but in dread. Hard sharp barks, like someone banging coffin nails in.

—So Nan knew she was going and she had a plastic bag ready to go over her head so she didn't squirt vital liquids from some unusual orifice. It's not as if she wanted to put us to any trouble by dying. She'd bought incontinence pads—kind of nappy-style undergarments on that last trip to the hypermarket, on the way back from what she always called the *hospitable.* That was one of her signature little jokes—because however hard they try, it can never be that—death can maybe, but not a hospital.
—You could call it a passing place.
—A passing place?
—The hospital.
—Well whatever it was, fire-trial, written test, whatever, Nan passed—they let her out!

—So beyond her bed, in a drift of watercress and flag irises with cropped and nibbled leaves which twined through the spokes of its wheels, was parked her heavy-duty wheelchair, which looked like it was built from scaff-poles and retreads. You could hear a babbling brook.
—You too, delirious? I asked.
—Or not delirious enough. No, but she was highly suggestive, she said. It was all there, live, in front of you. You could see & smell what she could.

It was harder to hear her now. Her voice was drowned by harsh raspberries blown by twin motors nearby. Keeping her mouth open, so as to be ready to start again when the time came, she paused her story.

—Death! I shouted, above the noise.
—Death?
—You know, I shouted, how within the last century, her scythe went blunt from over-use?
—Blunt?
—So she invested in one of those.

Because paired sextons, in orange jump-suits with chunky brass zips, and red plastic helmets, stalked amongst the trembling cushions of bramble engulfing the graves. They were waving identical strimmers like mine-sweepers, in unison, over the straight-faced dead. Each wore aviator shades.

She took a moment to understand, then made the face of someone laughing falsely, her hand fanning her lips.

—The mass-production of murder, I shouted. The maxims of Henry Ford applied to killing. It comes in a choice of colours—black. Though on reflection, I added, still shouting—though the noise was dying now as the strimming receded—perhaps the twentieth is not the last century after all. This century is really the last.

But my friend was grave. She was not so interested in what I had to say, however witty or universal. Or insensitive. And she wanted to finish saying about what—her Nan's death. The clever-clever and abstract of less interest than the felt and real. When the farting engines were finally quieted by distance, she went on—

—She'd bought a polythene builder's dust-sheet to protect her dimity valances. She wanted mum to have those. Her mansion flat was cold as iron in winter despite all the flowers and bees, and the council, tipped off by the practice administrator, wanted her out. The theory was they'd decant her into sheltered housing, only they didn't have any. Also, she wasn't paying the council tax, despite having all that lolly stashed with the *Co-Op*. She had a mental block about it, but the bright red ink of the dunning letters distressed her terribly. You see, pet, it's a matter of principle! she said, and she didn't pay, so more letters came, and threats. I defy you, she said, but they didn't even know what she meant.

After the war-grave department of the graveyard, with its geometric ranks of milky headstones, we came to the fractured and bucking flight of steps which led down amongst Buddleia and ferns to the immense cast-iron gates, furred with rust, of the catacombs.

—The catacombs!, I said. They've hollowed out the earth, beneath the grass, but left the graves there, so you can walk amongst the stacks of dead, as in the unconscious of a Dante or a Spencer! Stanley, that is.
—Until you lay yourself down amongst them for a rest.

But leaving catacombs and resurrection dreams behind us, we now entered the *Rose Garden*, set with rank swarms of spindly brownish rose bushes, parallaxing hypnotically away. You scattered the ashes of your beloved on the roots of a particular rose, so that they could be taken up into the blossom, and a bee fly away to some glass hive with nectar and pollen made from a pretty ankle or tongue. It was better than worms and stinks in the dark though, because of the fossil gasses used to burn you, not so green.

—The carer came morning and evening, and the district nurse looked in every which day. It's all over, bar the shouting, was what he (nurse) said after Nan died. The room was perishing. In the grate was a fire of smokeless-coal eggs, across which flared pulsing shadows and glows, and which, when he drew open the drapes and the winter sun flared in, went dove grey. Three days later, Chérie also died, her dog I mean. 'She lived a while, liked it not, and died.' *Here!* my friend said.

Because, amongst all the other rose bushes, we had found Nan's particular rose.

And my friend showed me a flesh-coloured plaque at its foot, grainy with gaudy crystals, & wrapped against the elements in neat plastic film.

VIOLET
Grandmother
Mother, Wife
In that order

—Catty!
—No, she explained, she really did love me the best.
—Did she have to spell it out?

—We found it, she said, the plaque I mean, in her chest freezer. The order of service she'd left on the breakfast peninsula, written in that beautiful loopy school-house script. *Jerusalem*, and the *Nineteenth Psalm*, Callas and one of those weepy late quartets by Ludwig van B, as she called him, probably ironically, though you could never tell, never can, perhaps, even. Plus the guest list, hilariously past its sell-by date because mostly dead. A wake of ghosts.
—A quake of them.
—She thought of everything, not just the pre-paid funeral, you see. She also pre-paid a fortnight in the Philippines for Uncle Jeff, Mama and me, as we were to discover only later, at the bottom of the freezer, and, only, I never went, couldn't face being stuck with the two of them. That was months back and they're still not home, but I did get a postcard from Mama saying her mobile was nicked but not to worry she was having a ball.

—Mama's a loon. Doolally, know what I mean? She's still very pretty, so. She's always hamming it up—wheezing out laughs over a fag & coke. She's hard to describe because it comes out brash, but that's just who she is. It was super-embarrassing when I was little—I knew she was common. Uncle Geoff too—celibate and hating it, but that making it *impossible* for him to shower or get a haircut—all he needs is a mercy-fuck & a make-over—he's actually quite handsome if he washes his hair.

—So my guess is they're both on a sexual tourism trip, an awakening. Geoff's having a ball in his own quiet way and making up for lost time. But sometimes it's as if it's Mama who's died (God forbid) and Nan's just gone home to the Philippines where she used to live, drunk with happiness to be back. Even if you saw them die, but especially if not, it isn't real. Only missing them is, which feels like they're blanking you.

Beside Nan's name on the glossy plaque was a clip-art wine-glass, two onions, and a stylised mound of laser-etched mussels; and beneath these was this—

sweat onions in butter with garlic
add moules and hot-fry till open
add glass of white wine or sherry and optional cream
simmer for ten minutes, enjoy it with a crisp white wine
eat the closed ones and you'll end up like me

—I'm sorry! my friend said. Her face was red, her nose was running, she was eying my shirt.
—She's so cool! I said.
—Yep, she said. I know. She was, very.
—Up against our debased and strimming *Death* who sports, under a dirty habit, scrupulously ironed black y-fronts loose about the leg-holes, it's revolutionary, a unilateral declaration of defiance.
—I defy you, she said.
—Yes.
—Are you hungry? she asked.
—Are you?
—Yes. But I'd like something healthy.
—We can make it!
—I know that.
—No, the *moules!*
—Ok, she said. I've been meaning to. I'd like that very much.

So that now, inside the hypermarket, seeking ingredients—the subtle orange air of the aisles and implausibly intricate mounds of product felt improper. Rosy meat, pasty bread, sallow cheese, psychedelic pillows of snack-food and folksy cartons of juice. A reductionist's take on the riches of a fruiting universe, as if deconsecrated and reconstituted.

Stalking the aisles were weary shop-goers, obese or skeletal, seeking the absolution once taken kneeling at a confessional.

—*Second call for contract cleaner to aisle number 19,* we heard, as if aisle 19 *(Canned Fruits and Soups)* were the departure gate for some tinned but cheesy paradise—the Philippines, perhaps.

—Now libraries are all closing and churches locked, she said, nailed-up, even, hypermarkets and malls are where it's at. And hospitals, of course. Fine places for sauntering in, so long as you don't need to buy anything, or aren't sick—or maybe are, she said.
—The *flâneur,* I observed, who used to haunt the arcades of Paris, Prague, Bucharest, has retired to that offspring of Lady Chapel and diorama, the cheese aisle ...
—But always remember the *flâneuse.*

She had made a basket for the garlic, butter & onions from the grass-green stomach of her sweater, revealing a small belly and sunken navel beneath her shammy-leather popper-shirt.

—Here *we* doze, I said, on catering-packs of toilet-paper and graze at the deli-counter or in the bins out back. When the weather's fine we squeeze between cars parked in the herringbone pattern of boxed dates, and when dull leaf through magazines, red-tops and the so-called *quality* press, obtaining a glimpse of popular delusion, corporate sweet-talk, multinational greed, municipal dreaming. To wind down we catch *X-factor* or *Paranoia* in the HDTV aisle. We are always almost checking out. The hypermarket, godless, artless, and inducing a passive frenzy, is ...
—It's called grandiloquence, she said. And you, her finger tapping on my nose, are an ineffectual slob.

Edging amongst gridlocked trolleys with the joyous verve of *palaeos* we hunted ingredients, and were not above lifting real-live-lemons, which we could not locate, more from mischief than indigence, from another shopper's unwatched trolley, substituting *Jif* which we could. Then, we went to wait at the clogged self-service checkouts.

—Reminds me of *how to snatch a chicken,* she told me.
—That's a bit random?
—Where the woman steals a chicken by putting it up her snatch in a Russian supermarket on *YouTube.* But first she smells it to see if it's good. And asks the other shoppers to smell it too. In the end, security comes.
—Talk about creative up-cycling!, I said
—It's enough to give shopping a good name.
—I heard, I said, in Russia their lives are unchanged by the coming of cronyism, and are still all queuing. They used to queue for a tram or a jar of pickled gherkins bobbing like turds in liquor, now they queue at airport security and the *Ikea* checkout.
—Hey, just like us!
—Or the gas station or on the jammed expressway. Otherwise unchanged.
—Yes, I see all that, she said. But they've phased out the death camps, for now at least.
—Instead of scythe or strimmer, death opted for the handy sickle-size, I said.
—Used it, it was quicker, to shove them over the edge as well as to hammer & slice them.
—And someone also said, I said, that to be a writer you had to write a novel about smart factory-workers with an incompetent boss, and next a novel about brave teenage boys dying to bring Leninism to the Afghan proletariat. Then you could join the Writer's Union and be a writer. *Praise power in language it can understand*—that's socialist realism, they said.
—And under democratic cronyism, like us, she said, it's the same, only you *praise the people in language they can understand.*
—It's the same!, I said. Praise the people in language we can understand. It's capitalist realism. Not at all how art used to be, when the task of the artist, as someone put it, was to bite the hand that feeds it, though not too hard.
—No, not too hard.

The light in here whirred and fluttered, not like butterfly, but fly. It was flaring, unreal. Not a fossil light, from ancient summers, but chemical, malevolent and arcane. It insulted your eyes. Beyond the orange-themed in-house canteen with its *Formica* walls patterned in retro ink-starved block-print motifs of the nineteen-seventies, there were picture-windows which gave little natural light this deep. Was something wrong with our existence—but we didn't know whatever had gone was gone.

We didn't miss it, yet were impoverished and wronged and felt *that*—just as much as if there were no more birds.

It was that our world was not exactly monochrome, but the only added colour was a muddy orange—with a few flashes of living green. All that was left was to love—but it was a damaged love, spoiled by its setting, a brown-out in the sphere of feeling. Even Cupid dirtied by the city. Sullied. Smutty cheeks, a smutty mind. Our life was confined not only to a minor key, but a compromised one, in some forbidden temperament that could only express misery and not joy. Whilst around us, thrown-back from loving onto eating & wearing, fatigued shoppers, the docile & the livid, their eyes starting in anguish, their cheeks swollen or clapped, paced the aisles of plenty seeking a release which still played hard to get. Everything was the same, with a mask of difference, of fashion, under which, with no intervening face, lay the skull of mass-production. It was shape-shifting in the domain of products which, like *foi-gras* geese, we were force-fed. And I had the disgusting inkling, when I noticed the scuffs in the sheen on the grey vinyl floor-tiles, that this place had opened some kind of commingling communication with the hospital so as to properly coordinate the incubation of unhealthiness. Crematorium, hospital, hypermarket—a lethal trinity with a dying fall, whatever that irritating *cliché* is supposed to mean.

Because I think what I was coming to see—and sorry to be so slow—was that the hospital was more a place of death than the graveyard, and the hypermarket than the hospital. Death is just death, but living death is a hyper-death—and this *existence* of hypermarket, car-park & traffic-jam, with their poisoned skies & poisoned dreams was that. Where'd we hidden all the joy. Had it been used up? Polished off? Even *how to snatch a chicken*, beautiful & hilarious though that was, in using the hypermarket's weight against itself as performance art, was also squidged by that weight—was confined in its joyless dimensionality. Becoming an *ersatz* joy, flattened—the ghost of a joy—like the ghost of a grubby pigeon or a rat. Like all ghosts it afflicted you, but was it there? Or was it just the scent of a raw chicken, gone off in the chiller, which doesn't smell right. So that, like a flower that gets the crimson and the blue it needs from mud, we were trying to assemble beauty from ugliness, stink & greed and use it to escape. But, from this sorry, morally drab place, was there such a thing as escape?

Or would it be like this forever.

—Something in us is nauseated by the pre-formed structures which mould our tenderised lives. Hypermarkets, hospitals, I informed her. What a downer!
—I can see that, she said, her widened eyes regarding the distance. You know, she said, not looking at me, we came here before she died.
—You said.
—I didn't want to, but we had to. *I want to go shopping!* she told me, most gruffly, so that I thought she meant chopping with an axe. But why, I asked her, I can just nip out and get you stuff. I can forgive them everything but the execrable food!, she said. It's *state food.* Would you like it? *Nationalised food.* So I just want to go shopping, dear, see? Nan, you're normally not like this, I said. You're normally like *when Nan was a little girl it was just mince and soup, soup and mince. With a nice bit of dripping for your toast.* Don't change the subject, I want to go shopping, she wheedled quietly. It's like what've they put you on, they've given me back a different Nan, I said. *But I want to go shopping!*

—Well we can't and that's final. The dishy doctor—that exuberant sports jacket and jazzy tie, matching his off-blue eyes!—said to get you straight home for a nice mug of *nescafé* and put your feet up. *My feet've been up for two bleeding weeks I want to go shopping,* she said, speaking slowly and clearly in the most sinister manner imaginable. Then she suddenly shouted *I want to go shopping!,* which gave me such a fright, and with such ferocity that her voice melted and tore into the most scratchy, razor-grained fabric of noise.
—They're crafty old devils, they behave different, smell different, wear different clothes, so we become convinced they're from another species. But they're just us in a year or two, or were us a few years back, I explained. That goes for the dead too.
—Yes.
—I've often said, I added, but I'll say it again, that just as every teenager is convinced they're gonna die young, as death approaches the idea we're mortal fades. Kinder that way. Death is just loss of the last illusion, that of life.
—Yes, but not in her case. It was as if her trip to the hospitable and maybe the screamer in the next bed had opened Nan's eyes to her own mortality. So now she had wheels on, as she put it, she said.
—Yes, and was attempting to out-roll Death, who was inching along behind in a Torquemada shawl, with gold teeth, lank hair, black nail-varnish, a pallid face and an ebonized Zimmer frame on which she turned acrobatic tricks. Because it's not dying that's stressful, but the fear

of fucking up the face-off with death. The superstition that there's some more or less way-out way out, but what is it? And since you've forgotten, you just rummage desperately in some old sack for extra time.

—Well Nan, we aren't, I told her. Her response was with her bony fingers to brake one wheel so that, almost toppling, we slewed round to face the pedestrian entrance to this place, which is as you saw coloured a washed-out tangerine and has a tubular galvanized steel portal inscribed with the letters of the word *W E L C O M E* above it. I want to go shopping, she said defiantly. No!, I said. No way! *En Oh.*

And, finally!, in the here-&-now it was our turn to check out as we passed our ingredients across the glass panel to be spangled with revolving red lines. It was characteristic of reality that it happened on several planes but all at once—the plane of now—graveyard, hypermarket—and the plane of then, recounted—hospital, death. Sometimes the planes merged in space, if not in time—hypermarket, graveyard, and Nan's *Peabody* flat where we'd go after to cook our *moules.*

—Once she'd got her way—she was always going to—we tried it in various ways, she said. First I pushed her in the wheelchair and she pushed the trolley in front, but the trolley kept veering off and colliding with the orange plastic fascia where the prices are.

—Next, she wheeled herself and I wheeled the trolley, but she grew tired, and like the primate she was, shook her twisted hands loosely and bitterly on the end of up-raised forearms. Finally I pulled her from the front like a pony between the handles of her chair as, facing backwards, incapable of prescience though gifted with hindsight, she drew the trolley behind her, snaking mildly.

The same strimming sextons from the graveyard earlier, in their orange overalls and aviator shades, were in the line behind us, their lower legs sprinkled with *appliqué* nettles, grass blades, bramble leaves, though less and less as you went higher, so that a living, matted green shaded to milky orange. Each carried a tortilla chicken-wrap and a transparent plastic bottle of *Diet Coke.* The supermarket a modern take on *les nourritures terrestres.* With the self-importance of functionaries faced with an imponderable public, with a crispy *hauteur* they blanked us.

—*Did you insert your coupon? Insert cash or press pay with card.*

—Do shut up, said my friend, not to me but the other machine. And she spat out some coins on the bar-code reader's glass—she'd been sucking them, & clinking them with her tongue on her teeth—Psyche intent on a trip to hell! Because, amongst other things she used her mouth as a purse. She imagined this subversive, even *engagée,* as if to ironise that money was something you could eat. So I claim, at least.

—Nan squawked for us to stop to choose some packet or jar. We were causing such hold-ups in the aisles that, like in the contra-flow sections of a motorway when there's a free breakdown service to keep things moving, a deaf-mute servant of the supermarket assumed the management of our trolley, and we were able to shop freely at last, liberated from practical difficulties. *Bravo!* said Nan. *Shop till you drop, no?* she added, tapping a twisted finger slowly against the side of her dry, freckled nose.
—*Après moi le déluge,* I explained, but in the meantime, with food and sex, and more if we are foolish, I said, we face down death.

—Strangely enough, I also thought—as Nan rolled valiantly beside me, said my friend, facing down her own doom with an *I want that, and that, and that!*—of her shrivelled womb. As an egg inside my foetal mother's body, I had been formed in Nan's womb. Hadn't I? Isn't that biology? And that seemed mystical to me.
—Yes.

—So then, our kindly deaf-mute assistant indicated with graphic hand signals that he had a pressing call-of-nature. So I took the trolley again whilst she wheeled herself, her twisted, bony hands pushing on the plump rubber wheels.
—Now, I announced, I see some kind of formal antithesis between hands and wheels, as between clouds and airliners say, as opposed to the mysterious congruence, already noted, between hospitals and supermarkets, or that between car-parks and graveyards, or consumption and carnage.
—And she got in this terrible mood saying *I want that, and that, and that,* and she was kind of barking at me, which made me jump, and I had to reach down all the things she wanted. I didn't have the heart to tell her that, judging by what the dishy doctor had drawn me away from Nan to confide, with exuberant gentleness and feeling, she wouldn't be needing much of this.
—In fact, it's equidistant between hospital and departure lounge, really. Frenzied temple of neither disease nor flight, but tasteless, toxic food.
—Cherries, *Trex,* bagels, hundreds-&-thousands, pea-shoots, Armagnac,

doilies. And when I said *but Nan, you'll never be able to eat it all,* she said, *Yes, no, whatever, not that, but I want that, and that, and that!* Sun-dried tomatoes in olive oil, anodised flan dishes, *crème fraiche,* buttermilk ... — she was yapping at me like a Chihuahua and I had to keep reaching things down. It was terrible. She went haywire. *How will you eat it all, Nan,* I asked, *It won't even fit in the chest freezer.* And she just said *and I want that, and that, and THAT!* She was kind of grunting and shouting. Slavering. It frightened me. So anyway, we went to pay, and there wasn't room to unload it all onto the conveyor-belt, and it was all banking up at the other end before I could get it into the bags, and I was worried it would not all go on her *Co-op Ethical Debit Card,* but it did.

—She's brilliant! I said. It's *all* about dying. This is what she was saying. She was refusing to die by exhibiting a doomed greed. Consuming was an antidote, consumption having replaced of religion, just as travel has art.

—Or else warning me. Gather ye chattels while ye may, she said.

—It's Rochester's *Lead her to death and make her understand, After a life so supple and so strong, That all her life she has been in the wrong,* or something.

—Yes. All of us get it wrong, it's only a question of choosing how. And if you have to get it wrong, why on earth would you want to get it wrong in someone else's way. No?

—Anyway, she said, on the way home we were so laden up with these mud-orange bags, she had them piled up on her lap on the wheeled chair so except for her stick legs sticking out you couldn't see any sign she was under there. She had her head turned hard-right so as not to be smothered by the bags mounded up on top of her.

—Like the friable soil of a grave.

—And I had bags hanging from each of my arms and from the wheelchair handles, but that still left the one with *Trex,* pomegranates and double cream. A kindly soul bearing an enormous portable crucifix—not life but death size!—painted in white emulsion & adorned with iridescent Christmas decorations, lifted the handles of this last bag to my lips while opening his own mouth wide and pointing into it, by which I understood him to indicate not that he was hungry, though it might have been that, but that I was to open my mouth and carry it like a dog a slipper. This made me salivate and feel sick, and my saliva was dripping into the bag, and running down my bare inner knees—I was wearing that green halter-neck in soiled & faded tweed—or above them my lower inner thighs as I walked, and the other bags kept tumbling off Nan's lap and spilling out across the road, and the cars—or do I mean drivers?—hooted viciously when I tried to pick things up, when suddenly the bags on Nan's handles made her tip stiffly and slowly backwards like an overloaded stroller. So, every time I let go she'd do a wheeled-chair wheelie, cushioned by but crushing all the bags at the back, which began to leak egg-white and mayonnaise, and the cars swerved or do I mean drivers and deliberately popped the bags of lamb's lettuce and spinach, and I was really horribly embarrassed should any one *see* me! And had no *idea* how to get her home with so much *stuff.* It was becoming *horrid!*

—*Horrible!* she repeated. After that she went downhill so quickly.
—Careering down those iconic steps in a *Silver Cross* perambulator with Pom, Flora and Alexander? She looked at me as if I was a bit mad.

—Your Nan, I summarised soothingly, sensing death, wanted (too late, alas) to taste the delights of unbridled consumption and the irresponsibility of the mortal. The tragedy of the commons expressed in time, not space. The spirit of *fuck posterity,* of greedy above all for what you don't need, dog-in-a-manager-wise. This is to be alive. Our self-expressive, poster-paint, cereal-packet and lavatory-roll primary-education has doomed us to extinction by famine, storm and poison, if only by teaching us solemnly what we already knew, how to accumulate. She tasted death, more steady and bitter than fear, on her tongue, and wished to efface the taste with olives, sun-dried tomatoes, *UHT* double cream and *Stone's Ginger Wine.*
—And also a 42" 1080p *Samsung* flat-screen HDTV, which fortunately they delivered themselves, just as we were finally getting back.
—Just as the *Eloi* in Mercury Wells, I explained, were in denial about death, which meant having no defences when terminally up against it, so *we* fondly believe retail therapy will not only make us happy and young, but immortal, I observed. Actually, like so much else it does the reverse of what it says on the tin, in, well, taking our lives. Interesting that consumption was a nineteenth century disease, just as much as a twentieth. Same name, similar symptoms, updated pathology, I noted.
—Mercury Wells? she asked.

Behind the sextons, the aisles and nave of the hypermarket were becoming increasingly congested. Two shoppers had started ramming one another's carts. One cart overturned, a carton split, a jar broke, and a glossy puddle formed of tomato-juice, vodka, clotted-celery salt and *bouillabaisse.* The victorious shopper was thrusting her trolley back and forth across the remains of the other's supplies, mashing them.

The defeated sat on the floor nearby like a rag doll, her back against a bottled-water stand.

—*Contract cleaner to aisle 7 please.*

—Trolley rage, she said. Don't you dare stare, it's ghoulish. Let's get out while we can.
—The proper end of a supermarket, this. As a setting, an ornate frame, for telling works of performance art. First *how to snatch a chicken,* then dodgem-trolleys.
—Yes.
—It's so stuffed, I said. It's like there are more people here than in the graveyard. More living than dead.
—I heard it's like so many people are on the planet right now, that there're something like only ten dead people, if that, for every living.
—And that maybe is why we're seeing less ghosts. Not enough to go round.
—Also it strikes me that everyone who was ever going to live is now living, and the whole of future experience and human time is being used up double-quick in these last few generations we happen to be in.
—*Fuck posterity,* because there is none, I said.

—So Nan had to get home to catch *Celebrity Come Dancing* on her old box-set and was egging me to go faster and faster, but I could only mumble-mumble because I had this bag swinging from my mouth, but I did try to run, stooped double over the low handles of the wheeled chair, the bags swinging in different directions like polyethylene dugs. She missed the opening credits, but caught the meat of the broadcast, her specs illuminated by revolving couples, and was easily in time for the revived *All Our Yesterdays,* which came on after. She was able to watch that on the new flat-screen which came just as *Strictly* was ending and was, surprisingly, a *doddle* as she put it to set up. So I left her there, seated in her electric massage arm-chair, her teeth set in a jam-jar beside her for the comfort, and tears coming out of her eyes. Interesting, incidentally, what that did to her face.
—What did it do?
—It made her look like an ancient & wise baby preparing for birth. The next time I saw her looking like that, without her teeth in, was when I've already told you she had her bedroom full of the nettles and her dressing room with stags.

The hypermarket car-park, outside, was ram-jam full, gleaming and shimmering. The sunken sun burned brown and purple zigzags in our eyes. Beyond the gates was a traffic-jam all down the cooling orange hill to her Nan's, and the melted, studiedly futuristic shapes of the cars, with their trapped and incandescent or comatose drivers, reminded me of those very molluscs, sweated in their shells, the dangerous ones, which as Nan's memorial tablet had warned us, fail to open.

—The crowd, I said, that veil, as Benjamin calls it, concealing the masses, viewed with such horror by Poe and Baudelaire, and even Le Bon, has become a crowd of drivers—the crowd has been mechanised, so as to augment its horror. It has become, in the *end*, a traffic-jam. This is what the world (love, music, nature, children, art) is ending for—a traffic-jam, spread thick on the burnt toast of our lives. Consequently, we too—now toast!

She made no sign she heard me.

—Take Volkswagen, I said, for instance, the People's Car, burnt offering of the Nazi regime with its collectivist dream of humouring the masses—Hitler the first beetle-owner! In being dastardly and deceitful even now, today, so as to get on with its proper business of killing people by means of those auto deadly sins of collision & emission, it discloses what a car *really* is. Honesty, or rather the intoxication of being true to yourself, sometimes being irresistible, however much you may pretend to falsity. Alcohol and motors having this in common—that they permit you to own who you are.

We came to a zebra-crossing and threaded amongst the cars.

—So, then, and, if we're talking honesty, I said, what about the horrible banality of car-park architecture! Low crushing ceilings; scents of exhaust, hot asbestos and sump-oil; near perfect absence of the living; gut-like pipes in playtime colours snaking around in the ceiling. And then the registration issues of high-frequency identity. Which is your floor? Yes! Which is your car? Yes! And then which is you? *Nooo!* Plus the phoney neon glare.

—All very interesting, I said, when viewed as the portal to shopping and entertainment environments. To atriums, to fascist-style parade-grounds for mall-crawlers; to musak-filled naves and their viscous, molecular crowds, prized at last from prized cars. And everything and everyone coloured a soothing, prophylactic pastel-beige. As if to suggest that hell, the carpark, is heaven's gate, and if we *can* leave hell and visit heaven, then by closing time we must be back, albeit laden with branded paper-bags in bright colours. Disclosing that ultimate in metaphysical truisms—that hell is not, after all, other people, but yourself.

She looked like she was thinking, and didn't reply.

It was a definitively joyless habitat—the graveyards and perhaps rivers representing the only asylum and relief. And the sky! How did we get here, stunted, grubby, like the flowers beside a motorway—but how? Just as religion, or ideology in general, is the absence of humour, more precisely its eradication by the un-hammed-up absurd, so a supermarket and consumption in general can be defined as the absence of joy, or its eradication by greed. And we were mired in this ersatz horror. And we couldn't even tell.

And getting your violet and green from mud? Maybe all that means is a child.

—So anyways, believe it or not, that was only two weeks later, she said. After she died they came for her very late at night, much later than they'd promised. Apparently, there was a *rash* of deaths. The undertaker herself told me snappily that she felt overworked and under-appreciated and quite frankly like *death warmed up*. Very unprofessional. She, the undertaker, had pimples—small white spots set in inflamed circles, and these seemed to revolve in their sockets so I had the horrible idea that she was watching me from them like tiny white eyes.

—It was dark in the street, she said, some kind of municipal brown-out, and the air was weighted down with an unseasonable frost, something to do with the brilliant stars that night, so strange for a city, set in a smoke-blue sky. But the telephone lines radiating in a 3-D sunburst from a telegraph pole into all the flats appeared to sing, perhaps with the storied love and lust they bore, and her body, already stiffening, would not go horizontally round the bend in the hall. So, for the last time, in her life I wanted to say, though it wasn't that, she was upright in her lawn shift, her mouth open, her nose sharpened and her eyes sunk and closed, a brittle waxwork being manhandled into place between her archetypal near-contemporaries, the Iron Lady and Her Majesty.

—Once out in the street, she said, they belted her onto a stretcher and slid it into a black refrigerated Renault *Trafic*. And she left home for ever.

And it seemed quite wrong that she left and we stayed, finishing off the last of *Amontillado* and gin, when normally it was always the other way round. Because normally it was us went home I mean. Something deep was wrong with the universe.
—Shifting ontologies, unstable, I told her. And unhinged.

—Mama couldn't wait to get the funeral over and done with, she said. In her will Nan said to gift her body to a home for stray dogs—*I've had my fun, now it's their turn.* This was just her having her normal little laugh, because the *Co-Operative Funeral Care* cremation was pre-paid. A lover of picnics, hi-jinks and thrifty frolics, Nan had requisitioned a wicker-coffin to be burned in, and I felt that today, her cremation day, she was here and now becoming her own picnic. The burning happened in an odd, tall, apse-ended room, smelling of white paint, burnt hair, and roses, with a high-level hopper-window on some kind of elaborate electrical ratchet-opening mechanism, furred with dust and far too high (the window I mean) to see out of except at some perfect, self-contained clouds and a brownish, feathered smudge like that which trails behind airliners.

—A red velour curtain on dinted brass rings and a mahogany-stained rail concealed the off-white oven-door, she said—off-white traditionally the colour of heaven.
—No, its pastel beige! And what your describing—it sounds like a camp!
—With the difference that Nan wasn't murdered in the most horrific and degrading circumstances imaginable.
—Death is murder.

I was doing all I could, you see, though I didn't understand this at the time, not to be worth her love. A clumsy lunge at freedom on the part of the unconscious. And she was quiet for a bit.

—No, she said in the end—she was picking up my lingo!—death is a mother who, like those snakes which dislocate their jaws to swallow an incipiently deliquescent crocodile, manoeuvres herself in such a way that, crouching like a speleologist, we have no option but re-enter her womb.
—Or death is just Medusa in a hoody, so you can't usually see the snakes. And, for pubic hair, worms! Worms!, I said again.

Worms! I liked that.

—So, she went on, the bio-degradable wicker-coffin went in on a checkout-style conveyor belt, the doors and curtains closed behind it, then moist and fierce sounds came out along with the roar of gasses, with a kind of ferocious verve, which I interpreted as that Nan was venting all residual emotion while, at Nan's request Monteverdi and Beethoven played, the authors of *La Belle Dame Sans Merci*, and the *Nineteenth Psalm* spoke—haltingly in that case, tearfully, and manifesting as Uncle Jeff, who accidentally on purpose referred to it as the *Nineteenth Hole*,—and I believe it was Callas or Kathleen Ferrier or somebody who sang a setting of Blake. All for Nan! I couldn't smell *her*, in particular, though I tried, that old scent of her I loved, I mean, it was *what* I loved, in that if I still had that I'd have her.
—Thinking that what used to be burned was witches, Saints and heretics in the days of *faith*, and now in our faithless times we burn our loved ones, even our pets, I said.
—Only, as you will recollect I have remarked already, she said with incipient asperity, perhaps mock, we don't murder them first. Except perhaps by making them miserable, by giving them the imaginary duty of consuming too much. Anyway, outside where we were instructed to mingle and examine the gorgeous floral tributes, Uncle Jeff asked if anyone could smell burning. Mama said no, though she could, she said, smell *urning*. Then she went on to *How much does a Grecian Urn*, and *How do you make a Venetian Blind* or a *Maltese Cross*, and so on and so forth. *Tout comprendre c'est tout pardonner*,—pardon my French, assuming, that is, you even understand it. I found it all agonising, but it was just a coping mechanism.

—Back at the flat we had cold cuts. *Cold cuts! Cold cuts!* And we got the giggles. And everything seemed wrong, until the most amazing thing, which you'll never guess. But it is was *so* amazing! It was amazing! *Amazing!*
—What?
—It was just amazing. It still makes me cry.
—What?
—When we opened the chest freezer to get something out. Sometimes I feel I'm naked, and someone is throwing buckets of cold water at me like they wash cars. That's how it felt.

She was whispering, very fast, so I could hardly hear her.

—At the very top, resting on the *moules* memorial plaque she'd already got done, was a cling-filmed cherry tart with a frosted post-it note in her

loopy script saying *Microwave this!*
—Wow!

She put her hand to hide her face, like in bright sunlight, and from behind it I saw water drip from her eyes, or else her nose or mouth. Above her hand, her temple showed, and a zig-zag appeared, figured in royal blue on her temple and the transparent outer edge of her cheek, which together with her ear had gone dusty and red.

—Beneath that were loads of cling-filmed *Tupperware* containers and old yoghurt cartons and freezer-bags, she went on. Of stews, puddings, tarts, pies, loaves, I don't know what, each with a neatly inscribed date for us to eat it, on a post-it note inside the cling film, she said, her voice distended by a hidden moan. An Advent calendar of meals. Cling-filmed mince and cling-filmed, chiselled chunks of soup. Also the recipe torn from a book, or snipped out of *The Lady* or *The Radio Times.*
—A dead writer can still look, with shifty eyes, out of miserable scry-holes cut in the pages of her books. Maybe the holes in every *oo.* Or in this case, a dead cook, out of the holes made by the birthday candles, say, or the holes in cheese.
—It was a humungous *Tupperware* and cling film fest. Which we slowly excavated over the next few months, until Mum and Uncle Jeff took off on their pre-planned holiday. Eating her food, that she had cooked for us, in that fatal fortnight between the *hospitable* and the prancing fawn when, even if *we* didn't, didn't really I mean—we knew it on paper—she must have known she was dying. So we were still going to be eating her food although she was gonna be *dead.* And that was her whole plan all along. All she'd wanted was a little posthumous joy. It was *weird.*
—Man is a cooking animal, says Johnson. Witchery, i.e. being a witch, is just a metaphor for cookery. Which is why they used to cook witches. Er...
—Something turned your stomach, but at the same time it was highly emotional and beautiful. *So* beautiful. Not about her, but us. I mean, all that *chopping* we did? She wasn't greedily doomed at all, she was hoarding for us, to eat after she died. She was making us *food.*
—Beautiful, but also something cheesy and something putrid. At the same time, it does seem to be some kind of existentialist gesture, such as embracing suicide as defiance and liberty. Declining the package at the door, whether you did order it or didn't. Your Nan, I feel, was manhandling or even tinkering with the enormities—re-engineering our takes on food and death.

—Yes. But why does people helping one another make me cry?
—Yes. But why?
—She'd made months of rolling feasts. *Savarin au Rhum avec des Figues et Fruits Glacées*, which, the idea of which, she'd got from some movie or book or something, which didn't freeze well though, as it turned out.
—The Egyptians buried food with their dead—this was just another way round, the dead cacheing food for the living. Some of the grain they buried is viable and has been sown and people are eating bread made from what comes up. So I'm told.
—Including once a week a fast! *Nothin doin you're on boiled water and lemon!* How did she do it? She couldn't even take a shit on her own. After the chopping-trip she never wanted me to come round except in the evenings. Smells gorgeous in here, Nan, what y'a cooking up? I was sure she was in there all day scoffing sun-dried toms and mozzarella pats in oil, and cackling over *Celebrity Come Dancing*, reflected in her specs *and* her eyes. But she'd never let on. All I got was a damp biscuit and stewed tea, and sometimes the odd *After Eight*.

—Now at the very bottom, once we had eaten our way down, like mice inside a *Wonderloaf*, six months of steady mastication ...
—And defecation. And urination!
—... to all but this pomegranate and passion-fruit tart, the last thing, which maybe we'll eat tonight, there was a pack of playing cards and three inscribed books, one for each of us. Mine was Dick Francis's *Dead Cert*. A very poor choice indeed. Mama also got a box of *Charbonnel et Walker* chocolates, a gold-lamé lighter case, a pack of multi-coloured *Sobranies* which are her favoured smokes, and a phial of pine bath-essence. And gin for Mama, rum for Jeffrey and a bottle of flavoured *Grey Goose* for me, only three quarters full and viscous with cold, also cling-filmed, in the flamboyant lustrous twirls of a boiled sweet. Oh and the tickets for that all-expenses holiday in the Philippines for once we'd finished. The Philippines, where Nan was seconded in the war as a WRNS telegraphic officer or something. That's where she got Mama. I mean from some random honcho out there. Maybe it was important to her to send Mama back. Return to sender. And finally of course directions to play the video message of Nan blowing kisses across the Styx in the form of a local canal and catching ours back in one upraised old-claw of a hand ...

But we'd arrived. She took out her key and let us into the common parts, then into her Nan's own ground-floor mansion-flat.

—And also a scarlet £50 note, cling-filmed, for each. Mama snapped hers, because it was rigid when it came out, like a frozen rose, but the bank took it anyway when she explained.
—The famous chest freezer, I said, that portable grave!

Because there it was, almost blocking the hall, just inside the door.

Nan's flat was cold, with a profusion of open doors all down a long corridor. The rooms had tiny cast chimney-pieces with tendrils and stylised stove-black hearts. There were parlour palms on *jardinières,* and coloured Scottish landscapes in flimsy gilt frames, their mounts scorched like skin by time,

In the kitchen—the bone-coloured elements of the cast-iron gas-fire, fretted like leached brandy-snaps. A *Baby Belling* with black splodges where the enamel had chipped. And a scroll-footed bath-tub under the hinged wooden side-board, which had a tattered oil-cloth in blue gingham with floral sprigs pinned down on it. Above it was an Ascot, subliminally religious, with its perpetual blue flame, which roared whenever you ran the hot, and sometimes jetted a forked flame right across the kitchen with a hard *pop!*

Cherie's damp fabric basket and plastic bone were still there. Her crimson lead, of thick fluffy rope, loosely braided like the halter of a horse, hung on the back of the flat's front door.

On the sideboard was Nan's photo in a mottled art-deco frame, also with tendrils and hearts, just like the chimney-pieces. Dating from her sojourn in the Philippines as—as my friend explained—a Chief W.R.N.S. Telegraphist attached in more ways than one to a R.N. liaison officer during the U.S. *Reconquista.* With her tilted cap, worn at the officially sanctioned rake, her collar-&-tie, her double breasted tunic, a serge skirt concealing rustling camy knickers, and high-gloss sensible shoes. She had the honour of telegraphing news of the fall of Manila to the Allies, and rode in a US Army 'jeep' through the aftermath, a handkerchief pressed to her mouth and nose, and bright tears meandering on her dusty cheeks, or so I was told.

My friend lifted the white coffin-lid of the chest freezer and leaning in deep, she took out a frosted tart and laid it on her Nan's melamine kitchen counter where, like some sort of affectionate cat, it twirled its smoke with the still wreathing freezer-smoke. Inside the cling film was the accustomed post-it. Opening it, my friend made a face of total delight, fanning her teeth.

—What does it say?, I asked. What is it?
—It says: *Mum back yet? Wink wink! Enjoy the tart, pet. I made it for you.*

A second post-it was still attached to the back of the first—

—P. S. Enjoy yourself. Death's a bitch.

So that Nan telegraphed wildly from our own future, a place she'd already gone. Forget ectoplasm and Ouija—this was an unequivocal communication—and above all the *Grey Goose* and pomegranate tart.

Now my friend spread a plaid synthetic motoring blanket on the carpet and we lay on our fronts on the dry, repellent fabric with our feet up behind us like children. The *Grey Goose* smelt of the yellow syrup used by men with origami forage caps in old-fangled milk-bars to flavour banana shakes. The blanket was still threaded with Chérie's bright hairs. .We watched a vintage horror-film starring Peter Cushing and Christopher Lee chosen from Nan's collection of video-cassettes. *Grisaille* movies have the effect of turning everything to the brightest moonlight, especially moonlight itself, and the video cassette added its own jerky grain. In the movie there was a monumental moonlit earthquake. Everyone knows that vibrating soil is fluid, so that coffins and bones (less dense than the medium) float to the surface, monuments sink and people swim for their lives.

The room smelt of nettles & thistles, honeysuckle, lime & old-man's beard. Warmed by a free-standing wrought-iron flame-effect electric fire we ate our *moules,* using the shells as juice-spoons, and then the posthumous passion-fruit and pomegranate tart with cream, and after a while we stopped the film and put some music on.

Bitter Fruit and other things.

—I remember, I remember a Lake Poets' dark dream of sticky comfort food, a nursery tart or something, but with a gash in it, a long wide wound, welling cherry-coloured blood, she said.

—Perhaps because—blood in the lake! Not all of them so honest that they talk about that, I said.

Recalling this now makes me cringe and sweat. Because the tart was finished, but the plate had left-over single cream on it, she rolled forward on her knees to lap at this. As she lapped, I reached out my fingers and touched her between her legs. She lapped faster. Through her tights she too became sweaty.

—But I think we should stay friends, she said, wiping cream from reddening lips with the back of her wrist.

And she lay on the rug on her back in her tights, which itched, hot and unpleasant, so she had to take them off, though she kept on her green jersey and poppered shammy leather cowboy shirt, licking pomegranate and passion-fruit in wide strips off the discarded cling film. Then she cling-filmed her face so she resembled a pornographers dummy, and made a forced smile, very wide, with plenty of plump teeth and terrifying eyes.

Her breath beaded in white globes inside a pulsing membrane over her mouth.

When I pierced her two nostrils by twirling a sharpened pencil, she took whistling breaths, and clung to me sensuous and despairing, like she loved me.

Her face inside the cling film went red, and her eyes an arc-lit blue, and all her teeth now swelled with the pressure with which she clamped her jaw.

I pierced the cling film over her mouth with the pencil, and kissed through the hole. Her tongue had this deep slot or crease down its centre, as if it was imperfectly unfolded. Like the hook in a song it made her addictive to kiss, especially with the wet hem of her tweed halter neck dress—which from trailing through the graveyard grass was still damp, and adorned with broken nettle-leaves—up around her neck, disclosing her navel and even her breasts.

—You know, if I get pregnant, I'm keeping it, she said, peeling shreds of cling film from her lips and from the dished or sunken sections of her face, and then slipping her head and then each arm out of her dress. Her hair ran down her forehead and her breasts like treacle. As *préservatif, mince et souple,* we used cling film, but it didn't work.

www.ingramcontent.com/pod-product-compliance
Lightning Source LLC
Chambersburg PA
CBHW030552310726
48979CB00011B/2131/J
* 9 7 8 1 9 0 0 3 8 9 0 4 4 *